FIC   8199
PRY   Pryor, Bonnie
      Mr. Z and the time clock

DATE DUE	BORROWER'S NAME	ROOM NUMBER
MAR 2 1 1991	*Bill*	25
MAY . 1 1991	*Brenda*	16
SEPT 29	*Carlos*	25
CT 1 0 1991 25		25

8199

FIC   Pryor, Bonnie.
PRY
         Mr. Z and the time
         clock.

DISCARD

SANTA ROSA ELEM SCHOOL
ATASCADERO, CALIFORNIA   93422

MR. Z
AND THE
TIME
CLOCK

Mr. Z
and the
Time
Clock

by Bonnie Pryor

GEMSTONE BOOKS

Dillon Press, Inc.   Minneapolis, Minnesota 55415

Cover illustration
by Chris Wold Dyrud

Library of Congress Cataloging in Publication Data

Pryor, Bonnie.
 Mr. z and the time clock.

 Summary: When twelve-year-old twins become owners of a
time clock, they begin traveling back and forth through time,
trying to solve the mystery of the strange Mr. Z who is a sinister
presence in their lives.
 [1. Mystery and detective stories. 2. Space and time—
Fiction. 3. Twins—Fiction] I. Title.
PZ7.P94965Mr 1986   [Fic]   85-25353
ISBN 0-87518-328-X

Dillon Press, Inc., 242 Portland Avenue South
Minneapolis, Minnesota 55415 8199

Printed in the United States of America
1 2 3 4 5 6 7 8 9 10 95 94 93 92 91 90 89 88 87 86

Contents

1 A Sinister
Antique Shop

When my twin brother, Jerimy, told me he had invented a time machine, I figured it was some kind of a joke. Even if Jerimy is practically a genius, he is only twelve years old. How could a seventh grade boy invent something that all the scientific brains in the world couldn't manage?

He had been acting strangely lately, but that was normal for Jerimy. Even if he is my brother, I have to admit he can be pretty weird. But so many other things were going on right then that I hadn't paid any attention.

It was hard enough getting used to living in a small town like Crystal Springs. We had moved here in August.

"You will have time to get acquainted with your grandpa," Mom had said when we moved into our new house, "and maybe even meet a few of the kids in town before school starts."

"I can hardly wait," Jerimy mumbled.

"I am sure you will make lots of nice friends," Mom answered. Her voice was confident, but she gave Jerimy a worried glance. "You have to give it a chance."

"Well," Jerimy sighed, "it will be nice to meet Grandpa. Grandparents are sort of obligated to like you."

Unfortunately, Jerimy was wrong. Our first visit started out well enough. Grandpa met us at the door with a big hug. He had a warm woodsy smell, and as his cheek rubbed against mine I could feel the leathery wrinkles caused by years of working in the sun. He was a big man, with almost snow white hair. He had been wearing a pair of wire-rimmed reading glasses when we arrived, but he tucked them away in his pocket, as though he was ashamed that he needed to wear them.

"Let me look at you two," he exclaimed. He touched my short curly hair. "Julie, you remind me of your grandmother," he said softly. "I think you would have liked her. But you should wear your hair longer. Girls nowadays keep their hair too short."

Even though I knew I looked better in short hair, I found myself wanting to apologize. "It used to be longer, but it's so curly that it's hard to take care of when it's long."

"Nonsense," Grandpa snorted. "What is a few extra minutes to look your best. You would be beautiful with longer hair, and wearing a dress." His face had grown sad when he mentioned Grandma. Now he took out an enormous handkerchief, and loudly blew his nose. "Tell you what," he said. "You wear a dress sometime and let your hair grow, and I'll take you out for dinner."

Although I hated to wear dresses, I nodded. He seemed

2

so unhappy, I hated to hurt his feelings.

Grandpa went into the kitchen and made us a cup of cocoa. An old wooden table was squeezed into a corner of the tiny kitchen.

"This was the table we had at the farm," he said, touching the worn surface. "Too big for this house, but I hoped one day your folks might want it." We followed him into a cozy living room and sat on the couch.

"Now then," he sighed, "it's about time that son of mine quit all that running around and settled down. Traveling around like gypsies is no life for children."

"We liked it," Jerimy bristled. "Besides, Dad was doing important work."

"No way to bring up a family," Grandpa grunted. "Never knew when I might hear that you had been kidnapped or worse."

I shivered, hearing Grandpa talk like that. Although Jerimy would never admit it to Grandpa, that was the reason Mom had talked Dad into quitting his job and moving back to America. Dad had worked for a big oil company in the Middle East, where we had lived for most of my life. Although we went to school and lived in the American compound, Mom had never felt safe.

Jerimy had never worried about it, and until just before we moved, neither had I. Life in the compound was pretty dull. We had a few friends, mostly other American kids whose parents worked with Dad. Since everyone moved around a lot, and most kids thought Jerimy was a little odd because he was always working on a science project, we didn't have any really close friends.

Once in a while Dad let us go with him on short trips to one of the villages. I loved those days, even though it meant staying in the car with the driver while Dad tended to business. It was on one of those trips that something happened to make me glad we were returning to the States.

Dad had finished his business early that day, and had finally given in to my pleadings to walk through the crowded marketplace. It was close to Mom's birthday, and I wanted to buy her something special.

Jerimy was quickly bored and would have bought almost anything. He wrinkled his nose, and I knew he would rather be home with his new chemistry set. But I loved walking through the narrow streets filled with people— women, some veiled and some in western clothes; rough dark men; beggars; children; and vendors. There was so much to see. Even the sounds and smells were exotically different. Squawking chickens, the smell of overripe fruit, and the exhaust from the sea of motorbikes added to the wonderful confusion.

We had stopped to argue the price of some beautiful cloth. It was pale blue, shot through with delicate golden butterflies, and I knew Mom would love it. But here, buying was a game. First you pretended you were not really interested. Finally a lower price was offered. You offered a lower price still. Then the seller would pretend to be offended. You would shrug and walk away. He would call you back, and the offers would start anew. Dad had almost come to an agreement when a sudden surge of the crowd pushed me away. In panic, I searched for a way back to Dad, when I realized that someone was watching me.

Remembering all the warnings I had been given, I scanned the crowd. Except for a few curious glances, no one seemed to be paying unusual attention. I tried to shrug off the feeling and make my way back to Jerimy and Dad. Neither one had noticed I was missing. Suddenly, a man loomed in front of me, blocking the way. He was terribly old, with piercing blue eyes that told me he was not a native, although he was dressed like one. For a second our eyes met. He reached one bony finger towards me. "It's you," he croaked, as I screamed and pushed past him.

Babbling with fright, I tried to explain to Dad. At last he understood. "Where?" he demanded, as his eyes scanned the crowd.

The man was gone. He had melted back into the crowd as though he had never existed, never stared at me with those knowing eyes, except in my imagination.

Now, sitting on Grandpa's sturdy couch in his old-fashioned living room, I remembered that taste of fear. Jerimy, however, still denied that we had ever been in danger. While I had been daydreaming, his conversation with Grandpa had nearly turned into a war.

"I don't think it's very nice of you to talk about Dad that way," Jerimy almost shouted.

"Your Dad knows exactly how I feel," Grandpa said. "Just like he knows I think children should be taught some manners. Maybe if you had been living a normal life, playing Little League ball and having a paper route, you would have learned some respect for your elders."

Jerimy ran his hand through his closely cropped blond hair. "I hate sports," he snapped.

Grandpa's mouth tightened into a hard line. "Sports might teach you something about getting along with others. You'll find that most of the boys in this town are interested in some kind of sport."

Jerimy shrugged. "Then I guess I won't have very many friends."

I sat there feeling perfectly miserable. This was the first time we had been able to know the rest of our family. Now here was Jerimy, starting a fight on the very first day. Yet I had to agree with him. Sports were okay, but Grandpa acted like it was a crime that Jerimy wasn't interested.

Grandpa, however, was finished with the subject, at least for now. He went on talking about other things, as if nothing had happened. From that time on, though, there was a frosty feeling between the two of them.

During the next two weeks, we were very busy getting settled in the house and buying school clothes. Towards the end of the month, on a miserably hot day, Mom chased Jerimy out of his room and suggested we ride to the park. I was glad. I thought we might meet a few kids that way, but it didn't happen. Everyone seemed to be with their families, having a final outing before school. We ended up sitting on the grass, feeding the squirrels some leftover bread crusts from the sandwiches I had made.

Everyone in Crystal Springs must feed the squirrels. They are so tame that they come right up to you. Jerimy tried to coax one into eating out of his hand while I leaned against a tree half watching, and half daydreaming. It was one of those lazy, do-nothing days that comes at the end of every summer.

Suddenly, I got a creepy feeling all over me. It was the kind of feeling you get when your parents let you sit up and watch the late night horror show all by yourself. You are afraid to look behind you. Even though you tell yourself it's foolish and there is nothing there, you can't quite make yourself turn and check. Maybe this time is the one time there is something really there. I had that kind of feeling, even though it was in the middle of the afternoon in bright sunshine, and in a busy park.

I sat there a moment, frozen in fear. I tried to convince myself I was being dumb. Obviously, Jerimy hadn't noticed anything. He was still talking to the squirrel. I looked slowly around, trying to find an answer for my fear. Some kids were climbing on the monkey bars, and under the picnic shelter I saw a family having lunch. Everything looked perfectly normal. Then I saw him. He stood by the path, staring at us. He was the oldest looking person I had ever seen. Yet even though he was some distance away, I could see that his eyes were an unearthly shade of electric blue. When he knew he had my attention, he nodded, turned, and shuffled off, moving faster than you would expect for his age.

I made a strangled noise in my throat and grabbed Jerimy. "Did you see that?"

"Darn it, Julie," Jerimy yelled, throwing down the crusts. "I almost had him. Now you've scared him away." The squirrel had retreated to a nearby tree, where he sat angrily chattering at the loss of his snack.

"Never mind that stupid squirrel. Did you see that old man?" I yelled.

Jerimy looked at the man rapidly disappearing down the path. He stood up, brushing off his clothes in disgust. "So? There was an old man. What about it? That's the second time you've got excited about some old man looking at you." He looked at me curiously.

It was like a shock of cold water hitting me. That's why I had been so frightened. The clothes were different; now he was dressed just like any old man might be, but it was the same man I had seen in the marketplace. There was no mistaking those chilling eyes. But how could it be? What could he be doing in Crystal Springs?

I told Jerimy, but he looked doubtful. "You must be wrong. But even if you are right, it's just a coincidence. Maybe he just happened to move here, too."

For a genius, Jerimy can be awfully dumb. "He just happened to move to Crystal Springs, a town of 6,000 people, halfway around the world?" I asked sarcastically.

Jerimy shrugged again. "It's probably not him, anyway. Come on, we might as well go home. That squirrel will never come back now, and I have an experiment I want to finish."

I sighed. "I'm sorry about the squirrel. I can't explain why, but that guy scares me." Now that it was over, I felt pretty dumb.

Jerimy didn't bother to explain his experiment. Even though we are twins, we are as different as night and day. We don't even look alike. Jerimy is tall and thin. I am short, and my hair is brown instead of blond like his. There is even more difference in our personalities. The only thing that interests Jerimy is science. His room is filled with assorted experiments in progress, various boxes, wires, and odd-looking contraptions. Even though Mom made him leave almost everything when we moved, his room is already so full you can hardly open the door. When Mom passes his door, she shudders, but she hardly ever goes in. She says it is too depressing after all the money they spent on the new house. Dad says if the garbage collectors ever go on strike we will be the only family without trash piled up. We could just throw everything in Jerimy's room. He would find a use for it.

I have to admit that my room isn't a whole lot neater. Instead of science, my passion is antiques. Every chance I get, I go to yard sales, second-hand shops, and antique stores to rummage around for things to add to my collection. Mostly, I find old bottles and books, but they are

9

interesting. I love history, and the things I find make the past seem all the more real. I often wonder about the people who lived long ago. Did they have the same feelings? What kinds of things made them happy or sad? I think about it a lot.

Jerimy can never understand my love for the past. He likes things shiny and new and says history makes him yawn. Actually, I think most people make him yawn. He is much happier in the company of his test tubes and microscope.

Since we are so different, you might think that we wouldn't be close, but that's not true. Of course, we argue sometimes. I could never begin to understand half of his projects, and it really irritates me when he won't try to make friends, especially when I know deep down he really wants to be liked. He gets angry when he thinks I don't stand up for myself, and he seems disinterested when I talk about some old object I've found. Even so, Jerimy is the one who usually lends me the money to buy an antique, and I am the first one to see all his inventions. We care as much about each other as any sister and brother can.

By the time we reached home that day, Jerimy had just about convinced me that the stranger in the park wasn't the same man I had seen in the marketplace. I tried to put the frightening figure out of my mind, but I couldn't help but look for him whenever I ventured away from home. Nothing, however, happened for several weeks following the incident in the park. Then one day Jerimy and I found an old antique shop on the way to the dentist.

We were going for a six-month checkup. Ordinarily, Mom would have driven us, but the car was in the garage being worked on, and we had to ride our bikes. When Jerimy said he knew a shortcut, I was glad. It was a long ride from home. Before long, we were on a street I had never seen before, in kind of a run-down part of town.

"That's odd," Jerimy remarked.

"What's odd? Did you get us lost?" I asked suspiciously.

"No, I know where we are. I bought some chemistry supplies at a little shop down the street just a couple of days ago. But I didn't notice that store." He pointed to a little shop squeezed in between a bookstore and a laundromat. In the front window was a handmade sign: *Mr. Z's Antiques.*

"We haven't got time," Jerimy said, reading my thoughts. "Mom will kill us if we are late."

"Just a quick peek," I begged. "It won't take long."

Jerimy shrugged. I could see he was a little curious, too. "I guess it wouldn't take long," he answered. "Look how small the store is. But we'd better hurry," he warned.

We parked our bikes outside the shop. A little bell tinkled overhead as we pushed open the door. Everything was covered with dust, and I had to hold my breath to keep from sneezing. Boxes, books, and old furniture filled every space, making it almost impossible to walk. Jerimy was ready to leave, but, in spite of the dust, I was fascinated.

"May I help you?" a voice rattled in my ear. I whirled

around, knowing, as I did, who it was. His ancient face was as wrinkled as a prune, and his head was topped by a few strands of wispy white hair. He tapped a bony hand on the counter as he spoke. Only his piercing blue eyes, beneath two shaggy white brows, appeared young. My heart pounded, and I shivered as though a cold wind had sent a chill through me. It was the man from the park.

"We were just looking," Jerimy said. "She likes old things."

"Do you, now?" the man wheezed, giving me an odd look. His voice crackled like dry autumn leaves rustling across a sidewalk. I shivered again, in spite of the warmth of the day.

"It is most unusual to find a young person who appreciates the old. But as you see, I am not quite open for business. I haven't unpacked many of my things yet." He waved at the jumble of boxes.

"Oh, that's all right," I said. "We are in a hurry, anyway." I started for the door, but he grabbed my arm.

"First, you must see my clocks," he rattled.

"Clocks?" I repeated stupidly. I was aching to get out of there, but I was also curious. There was something strangely haunting about the old man.

"Follow me." He motioned with one crooked finger toward the back of the store. Jerimy looked impatiently at his watch, but he reluctantly followed behind me. The man lifted a curtain revealing another room. This room was cleaner and contained clocks of every description. The ticking of clocks filled the room with a deafening roar.

"Are you Mr. Z?" Jerimy shouted over the noise of the clocks.

"Some call me by that name," he admitted. "Do you like my clocks?"

"They are very nice," I shouted. "But I couldn't afford any of them."

Mr. Z smiled a strange smile. "Well now," he said slowly. "I may have something you can afford. I have another clock, but I haven't had time to clean and repair it for display. I got it from—let's say—a traveling man." Mr. Z chuckled as he made his way slowly behind a glass counter.

"That sounds interesting," Jerimy said politely. "We'd like to see it sometime. But right now we are going to be late for our dentist appointment."

Mr. Z reached under the counter, as though he had not heard. He handed me a small clock wrapped in paper. "I can let you have it for a dollar," he offered, his eyes rather than his voice urging me to take the clock.

I had this creepy feeling again. One dollar was exactly how much I had in my pocket. It was almost as though he knew. I looked at the clock. It didn't look like any antique clock I had ever seen. Still, it was interesting.

"I'm not very good at fixing things," I said.

"Perhaps your brother would find it challenging. He looks like the sort of person who might be able to figure it out," Mr. Z responded.

Jerimy shrugged. "I could try if you want it," he told me.

Almost reluctantly, I pulled out the dollar.

Mr. Z smiled. "I am sure you are going to enjoy this clock. It is a very special timepiece," he added.

How did someone enjoy a clock? I wondered. Jerimy looked at me like I had lost all my marbles. I grasped the clock and hurried out of the door. When we at last stepped out in the bright sunlight, I gave a sigh of relief.

After a visit with Mr. Z, even a trip to the dentist would seem like a pleasure.

2 A Small Experiment

"I don't know why you let that old man talk you into buying that junk," Jerimy griped as we rode home from the dentist. "If you had a dollar, you should have paid me. You still owe me that dollar you borrowed when you bought that old bottle at the yard sale."

"I was going to pay you back," I tried to explain, "but something made me buy the clock. And it really is special."

"Humph," Jerimy snorted. "Use your head. Do you think if that clock was special he would have let you have it for a dollar? He probably knows it can't be fixed. He really is creepy, but you see I was right about him having just moved into the neighborhood. It was only a coincidence that you kept seeing him."

I knew coincidence didn't explain the creepy feeling I got every time Mr. Z was around, but I could see it was useless trying to make Jerimy understand.

Once we got home, I unwrapped the clock. "Wow, this clock is really different," I said to Jerimy. "Look!"

He gave the clock a quick, disdainful glance, but then looked at it a second time with more interest.

"What kind of clock is that?" he asked curiously. I shook my head. It was weird looking. In the center, the clock face was normal, but there was an extra hand pointing to the outside rim. Years were listed all around the outer edge. The numbers ran from 1,000,000 B.C. to the year A.D. 3000. A second row on the edge showed the names of the months, and a small window displayed the days of the week.

"You are the history fanatic," Jerimy said. "When did they make clocks like this?"

"Never, that I know of," I answered. "Maybe it's just some kind of weird decoration."

"Still," Jerimy said, turning it around in his hands, "it might be fun to see if I can fix it."

"Do you think you could?"

Jerimy shrugged. "I'll look at it and see."

He promised to start the next morning, but by then Mom had other plans for us.

"I've got a million things to do today, and I promised Grandpa Fenton I would take that box of things to him," she said after breakfast.

"What's in the box?" I asked.

"Those are some family things your father had—pictures, letters, stuff like that. Grandpa is trying to write a family history, and they might be useful. Why don't you two ride over? You can save me a trip," Mom said.

"Can't Julie go alone?" Jerimy complained. "I've got some work to do in my room."

"No. You've been buried in that room all month. School starts next week, and you won't have as much time to visit. Besides, I'm sure Grandpa would be hurt if he thought you couldn't spare a few minutes to go see him."

Jerimy made a face, but he didn't argue. He saved his grumbling for me after we started on our way. "I don't know why I have to come along. Grandpa doesn't want to see me, anyway. He wants a grandson who's interested in being a jock. Unless I join the football team or some other sport, I'm just a disappointment to him."

I sighed, knowing there was some truth in what he said. "He just happens to love sports. I'm sure he loves you. He just doesn't understand you. And you don't try to help him understand," I said.

Jerimy continued to complain. "He has everybody all figured out. Boys do this, and girls do that. And you just play along. Every time we go over there, you are so fake it makes me sick. Anyway, how could I help him—by wearing a football helmet every time we go to his house?"

"Of course not," I shouted, knowing what Jerimy was suggesting. Even though it was so hot that I would have been more comfortable in shorts, I had put on a skirt to please Grandpa. "But you know how important this family history is to him. You could try to be interested."

"It's boring. What do I care about a bunch of people who died long ago?"

"Look at it scientifically. All those genes made you what you are."

"You mean weird?"

I stopped my bike. "You aren't weird."

"Sure I am. Everyone thinks so. I guess that's what makes me so angry. I don't mind strangers thinking I'm weird. But a person's family ought to love you for who you are. You shouldn't have to pretend. I don't make you pretend to like science, do I?"

"No, but when you talk about it, I try to understand because I care about you. That's all I am saying. Be interested because it's important to Grandpa."

"He knows you are interested in all that history junk. It's you Grandpa wants to talk to." Jerimy rode ahead of me, but not before I saw the hurt in his eyes. "Come on," he yelled back. "Let's get this over with."

Our conversation seemed to cast a dark cloud over the visit. Grandpa explained how he was searching for the records for our family tree. He used old deeds, birth and death records, letters, and papers. Jerimy was restless, but the visit went smoothly enough until I told Grandpa about the weird clock. I left out the part about my strange feelings whenever Mr. Z was around, but I tried to describe the clock.

Grandpa looked interested. "Bring it over," he offered. "Maybe I can get it working for you."

"I'm going to fix it," Jerimy said, a little too quickly.

Grandpa sniffed. "I don't suppose you need any help?"

"No," Jerimy said shortly. Then, making an attempt to smooth out his abrupt answer, he stammered, "I work better by myself."

"Fine," Grandpa nodded, but his voice said it was not fine at all. "Well, I had better get back to work. Someone might be interested in this some day."

"Why didn't you let him help you?" I demanded when we started for home. "You hurt Grandpa's feelings."

"I didn't want to hurt his feelings," Jerimy said, "but I've got my reasons for not wanting to work with anyone right now. Besides, if we did work together, we would just end up in a fight. He would be talking about sports, like it's a crime I don't play."

"Why don't you just ignore him? Old people just get stuck on their ideas sometimes."

"Is that why you don't tell him to get off your back? You just stand there and smile when he's griping. At least I'm honest. He knows how I feel."

"I like Grandpa, even if he does gripe sometimes. Besides," I added, "who knows? When you're an old man, you might be as grouchy as Grandpa!"

Jerimy managed a laugh, and we didn't mention it again. We also didn't see Grandpa for a while because school started. Being in a strange school, Jerimy and I had lots to get used to. Even after school I hardly saw Jerimy. He disappeared into his room every afternoon and only came out for dinner. In the past, he usually gave me some idea of what he was working on. This time he was strangely silent. I was afraid to ask about the clock. I figured he hadn't been able to fix it and was embarrassed after telling Grandpa he didn't need any help. I had already decided that buying the clock had been a pretty dumb move. All I had done was waste a dollar. I put the clock out of my mind completely. That is why I was so surprised one Saturday morning when Jerimy called to me as I was getting up.

As I walked into the hallway, Jerimy met me outside his room. He was grinning. "Julie, I think I fixed the clock."

"The clock? You really got it to work?"

"Yep," he said, looking about ready to burst. "And I figured out why all those dates were on it. The clock is part of a time machine."

I stared at him, waiting for the punch line of the joke. But a look at his face told me he was serious. Like I said, for a genius sometimes he acts pretty dumb.

"A time machine," I echoed. "Come on, Jerimy, what's the joke?"

"I knew you wouldn't believe me," he sighed, "but I suspected what the clock might be all along. That's why I didn't want Grandpa to help fix the clock. I waited until it was all fixed to show you. And now it is."

"Is what?" I asked, trying not to laugh.

"Fixed. The time clock. Wait," he called as I started to follow him into his room. "Remember how Mr. Z said he got the clock from a traveling man? He said it kind of funny, and then he told us to enjoy the clock?"

"How could I forget?" I shivered a little, thinking of Mr. Z's grating laugh.

"It got me to thinking. I had a feeling he was trying to tell us something. And then he hinted that I would be able to fix it. There were all those funny dates around the clock, too. Anyway, I built this."

He walked across his room and flicked the bedspread off a strange-looking lump in the middle of the room. I had to stare for a minute before I realized what it was supposed to be. It looked like an entry in a soap box derby, minus the wheels. Actually, it was little more than two boxes nailed together. Carpentry is not one of Jerimy's talents.

I struggled not to laugh. "So that's what a time machine looks like. I always wondered."

Jerimy ignored my comment. "All we really need to do is hold the clock in our hands, and set the time," he explained. "But I thought we might be more comfortable with someplace to sit. I don't know how long time travel might take. Besides, in the movies there is always some sort of machine."

"The movies," I pointed out, "are fake. And," I added thoughtfully, "you said we. I'm the one who bought the clock. If it does work, it's mine."

"I fixed it," Jerimy glared. "You would have never gotten it to work. You wouldn't have even guessed it was a time clock."

"All right," I gave in a little, "then it's both of ours, but mostly mine. I get to pick where we go."

Jerimy frowned, then he laughed. "I'm always telling you to stand up for yourself, but do you have to start with me?"

"It's stupid to argue about it in the first place," I said. "There is no such thing as a time clock. It will never work, anyway."

"The scientist will prove its reliability," said Jerimy. "Where do you want to go? Would you like to see some cavemen or knights or pioneers?"

I thought for a minute. I didn't really believe for a second that I was the owner of a time clock, but it wouldn't hurt to play along for a while. "OK," I said finally, "let's start off slowly—sort of test it first. Maybe go back a day or two. That way if anything happens, it won't really matter—except I have to take my math test again." Suddenly, I grinned. "That's right. If we go back to yesterday, I could get an *A* on my test. I know the answers now."

"That sounds like a good idea," Jerimy said. "Starting off slowly, I mean. All right. I'll set the clock for yesterday morning."

Cautiously, I stepped into the rickety boxes. "You should have let me build this. I could have done a better job," I teased.

Jerimy ignored my remark. He frowned a little as he showed me how to set the controls. "Ready?" he asked, as he pulled a tiny knob on the side.

I held my breath. "Ready," I answered.

3 Dinosaurs at the Window

For the briefest of seconds I thought I felt dizzy, but it passed so quickly I wasn't sure.

"Well," I demanded, "when is it going to happen?"

Jerimy looked confused. "I thought it would happen as soon as I set the clock."

"I knew this was a waste of time," I sneered. "There is no such thing as a time machine."

I would have said more, but at that very minute Mom opened the door. "What on earth are you two doing?" she exclaimed. "If you don't hurry, you'll be late for school."

"But, Mom," I protested, "this is Saturday."

Mom chuckled. "Wishful thinking. You've got your days mixed up. This is Friday. Now hurry, before you are late for school."

Jerimy's grin spread from ear to ear when she had gone. "I did it!" he said. He grabbed my hand and danced around the room. "I really did it. Shall we go back to today? I mean tomorrow?"

23

I grinned back at him. "Shh," I warned, "Mom will be back to see what's going on. Why don't we just stay here? I'd like to take that math test again. It will be a snap now." A thought crossed my mind. "We could do this all the time—go ahead and find out the answers, and go back and take the tests. We could get all *A*'s."

"I already do," Jerimy said a bit smugly, "and so would you if you studied more."

"I do, at least most of the time. I'm just not very good at math. Anyway, just think of it. If you had a day that was really terrific, you could go back and have it again. I wonder if that means we could live twice as long?"

Jerimy frowned. "Say that again," he said.

"I just wondered if we could live twice as long."

"No, I meant the part about having a terrific day and having it again." He jumped up and tiptoed to the door. "Stay here, and don't make a sound."

"Why?" I asked, but Jerimy was already gone. Something in his voice made me do as he asked. In a minute he was back. "We have to go back. Now!"

"What about my test?" I wailed. "Why do we have to go back?"

"You can't take the test again," Jerimy whispered. "Don't you understand? You are already here. Right now you are at the table, eating breakfast."

A second later, it was Saturday again. "I still don't get it. Why would there be two of us?" I asked.

"While you were talking, I remembered something.

Yesterday, when I was eating breakfast, Mom came in the kitchen and asked me how I got downstairs so fast when she had just talked to me. Dad came in just then, and she didn't explain, but I thought it was weird because I hadn't talked to her that morning. I'll bet if you asked her, she would say that we thought it was Saturday, yesterday morning."

"I'm still not sure I understand," I said slowly.

"OK. Look at it this way. If we went back to yesterday, we would see all the people doing their Friday things, right?"

"I get it. That would include us. We would be there as our visiting selves and also as our Friday selves. Wow, what a weird thing. There goes my lovely idea about tests."

"I don't think that was such a good idea, anyway," Jerimy said. "It would have been kind of like cheating."

"I suppose," I sighed. "It's a good thing you thought of that." Then I laughed. "Imagine Mom's face if she had seen two of you and two of me eating breakfast. She would have thought she was going nuts."

"We shouldn't change anything," Jerimy said, his voice more serious. "What if we messed with something important? I'm not sure it's such a good idea to use the clock. Actually, I'd like to take it apart again and study it. I fixed it, but I'm not really sure how it works."

"Don't you dare. It's my clock, don't forget," I snapped. "You might not be able to get it working again. This is my chance to see history—all those things from the past that

I've only read about. Just think, I could step into the past!"

Jeremy sighed. "It's awfully complicated. What if something happens? Maybe we should tell Mom and Dad about the clock."

"No," I insisted. "You know they would just take it away from us. I'm going to use it. I'll go somewhere really great. You can come along if you choose, but, if you tell, I'll never speak to you again."

Jerimy sighed. Sometimes he can be a real pain. Still, I did want him to come with me. That is one reason we always get along so well. I think up the ideas, and Jerimy supplies the practical sense to keep us out of trouble. He might be a little dull sometimes, but he is a good person to have around if you need help. This time, though, I wasn't sure if he was going to help me. His forehead was wrinkled, and I knew he was worried.

"Come on, Jerimy," I begged. "It won't be any fun if you don't go."

Even though I did have a few new friends at school, I still spent most of my time with Jerimy. There weren't any other kids in the neighborhood, but even if there were, Jerimy would still be my closest friend. I think Mom hoped there would be some kids around when we moved here so we wouldn't spend so much time together. But our only real neighbors are the Petersons, an old couple who live across the street. Our new house is on the edge of town, not really out in the country, but where the houses are widely spaced. Luckily, Crystal Springs is small enough

that we can walk or ride our bikes almost everywhere—
that is, when I can get Jerimy away from his experiments.

For a second, I wondered what it would be like to have a normal brother, who didn't have ropes and pulleys strung across his room to turn off lights. A normal brother would be wild about an adventure like this and not think through everything. Instantly, I was ashamed. I was as bad as Grandpa. I wouldn't even have the chance to travel through time if Jerimy hadn't fixed the clock. A normal brother wouldn't have known how.

Jerimy nodded reluctantly. "I'll go with you, and I won't tell anyone. But you have to promise not to change anything. We must be very careful and just observe." When I nodded, he smiled. "Where, I mean when, do you want to go?"

"Let's go all the way back to the beginning, and watch things happen all along. Maybe we could see some dinosaurs."

Jerimy set the clock to the very end. "There weren't any dinosaurs by 1,000,000 B.C., but we might see some interesting early mammals."

"Where are Mom and Dad?" I asked as we climbed into Jerimy's time machine boxes.

"Sleeping in, I think. We'd better set the clock for the same time it is now when we come back. We wouldn't want them to discover us missing," Jerimy said. He checked his regular clock on the table.

I squeezed my eyes shut. "I hope this works. One million

27

B.C. is an awful long time ago."

I felt that strange dizzy feeling, this time lasting several seconds. Beside me I could hear Jerimy's ragged breath. My heart pounded, and a loud roaring noise filled my ears. All of a sudden the noise stopped. I waited a second for my stomach to settle before I opened my eyes. When I did open them, everything looked the same. We were still in Jerimy's room.

"What went wrong?" I asked.

Jerimy frowned. "I don't know. Something happened. I felt it, didn't you?"

I nodded.

Jerimy pointed to the time clock. "I set it right. Look."

The hand on the clock pointed to 1,000,000 B.C. "Well, it's for sure something went wrong. This house wasn't here a million years ago," I said.

"I'll turn on the radio," Jerimy said. "Maybe we can find out what day it is. Hey, does it seem awfully cold in here to you?"

"Maybe it turned cold last night. I didn't notice it before, though." I grabbed a blanket off the bed and wrapped it around my shoulders. "Hurry up and turn on the radio." My teeth were already chattering.

Jerimy reached over and turned the dial. "That's funny. It's not working."

"Maybe it's unplugged."

He checked the plug behind the desk. "It's plugged in all right. I wonder. . ." He flipped on the light switch. Nothing.

"You don't think the time clock did that, do you?" I was frightened, thinking of the whole house without electricity, maybe the whole town.

"I don't see how the time clock could be responsible," Jerimy said thoughtfully. "Wait!" He ran to the window and looked out through the curtains.

"Julie," he called in a strangled voice. "Remember what I said about the house not being here in 1,000,000 B.C.? Well, I was wrong."

I ran to the window. "I don't understand. How could the house. . .oh, my gosh!" I gasped.

The scene outside the window was like nothing I had ever seen before. The rows of maple trees that lined our street were gone. Instead, as far as the eye could see, there was nothing but ice and snow. Here and there a few patches of frozen earth poked through. Where you could see the ground, there were a few mosses and scattered, short bushes fighting for life.

"What have we done?" I cried.

Suddenly, Jerimy laughed. It started as a chuckle and grew until he was doubled over with laughter. I stared at him, wondering if he had lost his mind. I didn't see one thing funny about the scene out the window.

"Jerimy Fenton, it's not funny. Stop laughing, and figure out what we should do," I yelled.

"Don't you get it?" Jerimy hooted. "Nothing is wrong. This is the year 1,000,000 B.C. We are right on the edge of a retreating ice field. It's the end of an ice age."

"What about the house, the electricity?"

"That's what's so funny. There is no electricity because Ben Franklin won't be born for another million years. The whole house became a time machine. We took it with us."

"Mom and Dad are going to kill us," I moaned.

"We'll get the house back," Jerimy said, laughing again. "From now on we will have to use the machine outside. I wonder what Mr. Peterson would think if he looked out his window right now. There must be an empty spot where our house used to be."

I had to laugh, too. Mrs. Peterson is OK, but Mr. Peterson is a grouch. "He's much too sensible to believe in disappearing houses," I grinned. "He'll probably think we moved—house and all!"

Jerimy quickly turned the clock back to our time. In a second I felt that familiar dizzy feeling. But in the same instant, above the roar, I heard another sound. It was a short, high scream, and it came from the kitchen, the kitchen where our mother had unknowingly been cooking breakfast a million years in the past.

4 A Visit to the Future

"I just can't get over it," Mom said. "It all seemed so real. I have never had an experience like that." She shook her head. "I hope I never have a dream like that again."

I coughed, trying not to strangle on my Crispy Creature cereal, and hoping I didn't look as guilty as I felt. Across the table from me, Jerimy looked the picture of innocence as he buttered his toast.

"You must have fallen aleep while you were waiting for the coffee to perk," Dad replied. "You just didn't realize that you did."

"I know you are right," Mom said. She even managed a chuckle. "But that was the most realistic dream I've ever had. I even felt cold, and I heard this strange roaring noise. Just imagine, looking out the kitchen window and seeing a wooly mammoth staring back at me."

"Everything in dreams is supposed to have a hidden meaning," Dad said. "I wonder what seeing a wooly mammoth represents." He grinned slyly at her. "Maybe you are worried about getting old. You did just have a birthday."

Mom frowned. "I was forty, not forty million!"

"Actually," Jerimy spoke for the first time, "there is some evidence that the wooly mammoth survived until fairly recent times. It may have been hunted into extinction by early man. But what you saw was probably a mastodon. Prehistoric mammal bones have been found not too far from here."

Mom gave him a strange look. "I didn't see either one," she said. "It was just some kind of a weird dream, like your dad said."

I avoided looking at Jerimy while we finished our breakfast. As soon as we had arrived back in the present, we had dashed to the kitchen. We found Mom standing by the window, her face as white as a sheet. Thank heavens, Dad had been able to convince her it was all a dream.

"Well, enough about dreams," Mom said briskly. "I'm going to give the house a good cleaning and airing out today before it gets cold."

"Your mom wants to be sure she sweeps out all those dinosaurs," Dad said with a wink.

I still felt uncomfortable and kept my eyes lowered as I scraped the last bit of cereal out of my bowl. I didn't want Dad to see how guilty I felt.

"I've got some errands to do in town, and then I'm going to stop at Grandpa's. Anyone want to come along?" he asked.

I started to say yes. Because Grandpa was getting old, and his health was not too good, Dad usually stopped by on Saturday mornings to help with the heavy chores. Besides, even though going to Grandpa's was sometimes uncomfortable for us, Jerimy and I liked to go shopping with Dad. When Mom does her shopping, she comes straight home, but Dad always stops for ice cream or pop. This time, though, before I could answer, Jerimy did.

"Julie and I have to work on a project for school."

What was Jerimy thinking of now? I wondered.

Dad was not really listening. "Oh," he asked absently. "Do you need any help?"

I jumped up and started clearing the table, in case he asked any more questions. Jerimy calmly answered, "No, thanks. We are almost finished. We will be outside most of the time."

"Good," Mom said. "I'll be able to get more done with everyone out of my hair."

We waited until Mom had gone to the basement with a load of laundry before we carried the time machine out of the house and hid it behind some bushes at the back of our yard.

"Let's make sure we are out of sight from the house," Jerimy said. "I think Mom has had enough surprises for one day. If she happened to look out right when we disappeared, she would really flip."

Once the boxes were well hidden, Jerimy asked, "Where do you want to go this time?"

I thought for a minute. Even though Jerimy was worried about accidentally changing time and didn't think we should use the clock until we understood it, he had agreed to help me. Maybe if we started with something he would like, he would be more willing to go next time. Although I would have preferred to go back in time, I suggested, "Let's go to the future. I'll bet it's wonderful. Just think of all the things that might be invented by then."

Jerimy looked a little more interested. "How about all the way? To the year 3000?" he asked. "I wonder why the numbers only go that high?" he added, staring at the clock.

"Maybe that is when the clock was invented," I guessed. "I would really like to know how Mr. Z happened to have it."

Jerimy shrugged as we set the controls.

"What are you two doing there?" a voice asked almost immediately. We found ourselves sitting on the edge of a super highway of some kind. Before us, a steady stream of cars passed in both directions. I shouldn't really say they were cars, although I was pretty sure that's what they were. For one thing, they didn't have any wheels. Instead, they floated silently, about a foot off the road. It seemed strange to see all that traffic, and yet there was hardly a sound. I looked around the land that had once been my back yard. The house was gone, as well as the yard. Instead of open space, we were surrounded by a gigantic city. Tall graceful buildings were visible in every direction. Even the sky looked different, almost unreal. Then I figured out what it was. Everything, as far as the eye could see, was covered with a huge plastic bubble.

I was so busy gawking around at everything that I had forgotten the voice I first heard. Suddenly, I realized how silly we must look, sitting on the edge of the road in a couple of wooden crates.

"I asked what you were doing," the voice repeated. For a second I couldn't see anyone until Jerimy dug his elbow in my side and pointed up. There was one of the bubble craft hovering in the air above us. What I had thought were cars were actually some kind of low-flying airplanes. Out of the corner of my eye, I saw Jerimy hide the clock inside his shirt.

The machine lowered gracefully onto a small patch of grass, right where Mom's vegetable garden used to be. A man climbed out and walked over to us. He frowned.

"This is Country Day," he said. "Why aren't you with the others of your kind?" His manner was stern, although he seemed more puzzled than angry. I wondered what he meant by "our kind." He stared at our clothes. His own clothing consisted of a pair of shorts, made of a smooth glittery material, and sandals.

"We were just playing," Jerimy answered. "We are sorry if we're somewhere that we're not allowed."

"Playing?" The man spoke the word as though he had never heard it. He continued to stare at us.

After a long silence, he spoke. "I will have to take you to

the Director. She will decide what is to be done with you."

"Who is the Director?" I asked nervously.

"The supreme ruler of Centia, of course. She is the head of the council. Even one of your kind should know that."

So even the name of the town was different. And there was that phrase again, "your kind."

Beside me, Jerimy's hand moved to his shirt. "Want to go back?" he mouthed.

I shook my head. The future was scary, but it was also beautiful. I wanted to see more. "Not yet," I whispered, "but stay ready."

"Don't worry about that," he said grimly. As he watched the man, Jerimy carefully kept his hand in his shirt.

"You will follow me," said the man. He motioned to the bubble.

"What do you mean when you call us 'your kind'?" I asked.

"Why, children, of course. Surely you know children are not allowed out in the city." He climbed in the bubble and waited until we followed. Then he typed out instructions on a computerlike screen. He leaned back in his chair and swung around to face us while the craft lifted off silently and skimmed the road.

"You can call me Mart." The strange man smiled for the first time. His face was young and unlined, but I had thought him older at first because he was completely bald. I noticed him looking at our hair, not with envy, but more with curiosity. "Where did you find those odd garments?"

he asked. Although he spoke English, the words had a strange lilting sound that made it difficult to understand. I wondered if we sounded strange to him.

"We found them," Jerimy blurted out. "We wanted to dress up while we played."

"You spoke that word before," Mart said. "I am not familiar with it. What does it mean?"

"Don't the children ever play here?" I asked. In such a beautiful world, was there no time for fun? I wondered.

"Games," Jerimy tried to explain. "Pretending. Fun."

Mart still seemed puzzled. "I have not seen any as young as yourselves for many years. Is this something new the Masters teach in the lower cycles?"

I nodded, trying to bluff, but I had to ask, "Why haven't you seen any children for years?"

"The master robots do not allow the children to join the adults until they have finished their learning cycles," Mart said. "I completed mine, not long ago," he added proudly.

"You are just now done being a child?" I asked.

"I was forty two weeks ago," Mart said, "and I am now considered an adult. I have been assigned living space and a job. The Director herself appointed me parks assistant. I was on my way home from the required two hours work when I saw you."

"That's nice," I said weakly. "About your job, I mean."

"What do you call that clothing?" Mart asked. "It looks very uncomfortable."

"Jeans," Jerimy answered. "Everyone wears. . ."

"In the last learning cycle," Mart said slowly, "we studied ancient peoples. I heard that word then. Jeans were often worn before the great war. After that, of course, there was no land to grow the cotton, I believe that is what it is called. Yet these jeans, as you call them, are almost new."

He suddenly swung his chair around and changed the bubble's direction. I looked down at the stately buildings and parks as we passed. If Jerimy set the clock to go back now, he and I would have a terribly long walk, for we had been flying for several minutes, and I wasn't even sure of the direction. The time machine moved only in time, always remaining in the same place. We needed to get back to the boxes, somehow. I was sure that Mart was suspicious, and his world did not seem very friendly.

He swung his chair around again and faced us. He managed a faint smile. "I don't know who you are, but I do know you are not of this land. I am taking you to my living space. We will talk, and I will decide what to do. I am afraid the Director will be quite harsh if she learns of your existence. I am taking a risk to help you, so I would advise you to be truthful with me." His smile widened and, in that instant, I knew we had found a friend. "All my life I have been told what to do. I am even told what to think. Yet there remains something in me that wants to do something different. I think," he said, winking, "that I am about to have an adventure. Besides, I like you."

I sighed and shrugged. "You are partly right," I admitted. "We are strangers, but we do come from here. But the here we came from was a pretty little town with houses and lots of trees, and the kids lived with their parents and played. That was a long time ago. You see," I continued, ignoring Mart's shocked look, "we are visitors from the past. We came here in a time machine to see a future we thought would be wonderful. But," I added, lowering my voice, "I think we would both rather be home."

5 The Truth
about Mr. Z

I expected Mart to laugh or, at the very least, look doubtful. Instead, he sat quietly, staring at us through narrowed eyes, as though weighing the truth of my words. Finally, he nodded.

"I guess I knew it the minute I saw you," he said. "It just seemed so fantastic. For certain, the Director must not learn of your presence," he added. "She would surely try to prevent you from going back. Finding you here could mean death or imprisonment for all of us. Humans are wise to do nothing to draw attention to themselves these days."

A chilling thought entered my mind. "Mart, isn't the Director human?"

Mart shook his head. "Oh, the rulers look human enough. That is why one cannot be too careful. But they are not. A decision was made a long time ago that humans were not stable enough to rule themselves. You see," Mart said when he saw our faces, "there were terrible wars.

Something had to be done before we destroyed the earth, so my ancestors gave absolute power to the robots. Now I have heard there is a movement to return power to the humans," Mart said wistfully, "but perhaps it is only a rumor."

"Being ruled by robots sounds awful," I said. "I hope the rumors are true. I would hate to have a robot telling me what to do."

Mart sighed. "It would be very difficult to return humans to power even if that rumor were true. Robots are everywhere. Besides, there are many humans who would report anyone working for such a goal."

"You mean humans would tell on other humans—to a robot?" Jerimy asked.

"They would be rewarded, of course," Mart said. "But don't judge them too harshly. After all, we are taught from birth that this is the only way to save the world. Yet there is something in some of us that yearns to be free, to rule our own destiny—no matter what that is."

Mart reached into a compartment and handed us two hats made out of the same glittery material as his clothing. "I would suggest you put these on before we land."

"I don't understand," I said, obediently stuffing a hat on my head. "What are these for?"

"It might help to make you less noticeable," Mart said. He motioned for me to tuck my hair up under the hat. "I don't know what to do about the clothes," he added, as he turned back to the controls. He settled the bubble effort-

lessly in a small field. There were other similar craft nearby, and a steady stream of people walked to and from a
stark, white tower at the end of the field. "Take a good look
at everyone," Mart grinned, "and perhaps you will understand the need for a hat."

I stared out at the people. "Everyone is bald," I gasped.

It was true. Even the women were completely without
hair, like Mart, though they were still attractive in a
strange sort of way. The women were dressed in short
dresses of the same kind of cloth, mostly pale blue or
yellow in color. There was not a child to be seen, and the
adults looked nearly alike, as though they had been
stamped out of a machine.

"Why doesn't anyone have hair?" Jerimy asked.

Mart chuckled. "I know our ancestors had such a body
covering. I suppose people lost it when the city was covered. As you can see," he said, pointing to the dome, "we
are completely protected from the weather. And, of
course, it is so much cleaner and more attractive."

Did that make us seem dirty and unattractive because
we had hair? I wondered.

"What is Country Day?" Jerimy asked. I was glad he
changed the subject. Maybe we could find out something
that made us similar to the children of the future.

"Once a month, the children are taken outside the city.
I think you might call it play. They are encouraged to
exercise on that day. Our society discovered that children do better if they are allowed to have some free time."

"Only once a month?" I asked. "What do they do the rest of the time?" I was beginning to realize what a bleak life they must lead.

"The children spend their time in learning cycles with the Masters. Just as I did. Each cycle lasts a year," Mart explained. "When they have finished forty cycles, they are adults and may live in the city. Until that time, they must stay in their own section."

"If you are a child until you are forty, how long do you live?" I asked.

"Most of us live to be one hundred and fifty. Some reach two hundred," Mart answered.

While I tried to digest that bit of information, I glanced out of the window. I began to wish I was back home, safe in my own back yard. Going to a school run by robots for forty years didn't sound very pleasant. And never able to see your parents! According to Mart, babies were taken to the robot's nursery as soon as they were born. Who would want to live for a hundred and fifty years if life was so grim? Even with the beautiful surroundings, life in the future seemed awful. People walked quickly with their heads down. Nowhere did I see anyone smile or wave or even stop to talk. As I looked around, I tried to think of something to say to break the silence. "I thought you said this was where you lived," I said to Mart. "I don't see any houses."

"That tower leads to our homes. Only the public buildings are above the ground. The housing cannot take up valuable space that is needed for food production. We could live outside the city, but, of course, no one wants to live without the protection of the shield. It would be so unhealthy, in just that open air," he shuddered. He tapped his finger softly on the side of his nose. "I planned to take you to my quarters," he said thoughtfully, "but I see that would be foolish. Someone is sure to report us. I don't know where to take you, but we must not stay here much longer. People will begin to get curious. I am very afraid for you. Can you make it back to your own time?"

Jerimy nodded, patting the clock beneath his shirt. "If you can take us back to where we were."

"Perhaps that would be best then," Mart said unhappily, "though I would really like to talk with you longer."

"I don't understand why the Director would care if we were here for a while," I said. I was disappointed that we had seen so little.

"The Director and the council rule without jealousy, greed, or passion," Mart said, "and that is a good thing. But there is also no love nor kindness in their decisions. You see, time travel was invented about fifty years ago, and the Director outlawed it shortly after. The excuse given was that history might be changed.

"I think the real reason was that she feared travelers would bring back ideas about individual worth, and therefore, rule by robots would be threatened. The council looked for an excuse to ban time travel, and they found one. There was some kind of accident involving the creator of the clocks, and that was the reason they gave for confiscating them and making it against the law to make more. I see, however, that there is, at least, one more.

"The Director does not like to be disobeyed. At the very least, you would have to turn over the clock. If that happened, you would be caught in this time. How do you happen to have a time clock?" he asked as an afterthought.

"A strange man sold it to us," I explained. "He called himself Mr. Z."

Mart's face tensed. He gave a quick glance around as though afraid we would be overheard. "I think we had better go right away. I will take you back to where I first found you."

"Do you know Mr. Z?" I asked.

"Mr. Z was the name of the man who invented the time clock," Mart whispered. "He was banished from the city and sent to another time in exile. The rumor was he had killed someone."

Jerimy was the first to respond. His voice shook with excitement. "Now we know for sure it wasn't an accident. Mr. Z knew it was a time clock. But why did he give the clock to us?"

"You're right," I said thoughtfully. "He meant for us to have it. That's why he followed us, to make sure we were the ones. I remember when I first saw him, he pointed to me and said, 'It's you,' like he recognized me. But why? What makes us so special?"

"I am afraid I cannot help you. You will have to learn

45

the answer for yourselves," Mart said. "Be very careful." With a sigh, he added, "You must not come back to this time. If you have a connection, even a small one, with Mr. Z, you would be in grave danger. Take my advice. Go back to your own time, and destroy the clock. Forget you ever had it."

We flew back to the spot where we had first met our new friend. "Goodbye, my young friends," Mart said, a bit of sadness in his voice. "I wish I could have learned more of your world and shown you some of mine, for there is good here, too. But, at least, we have had this moment. I shall not forget you."

Our last glimpse of the future was Mart's hand raised in a wave. In an instant we were in our wonderfully familiar back yard.

"Now I know why explorers always kiss the ground," I said. "I never realized how wonderful it is." There was Mom's flower garden putting on a final show before the cold weather. It would, most likely, be the usual winter— the kind you shiver and shake through, wishing for spring. There would be no shield to protect us. Right then I promised myself I would enjoy each miserable day.

There was our white house, comfortable, and, best of all, above the ground. Here we were on a Saturday afternoon, with nothing to do but loaf around. Well, that wasn't quite true. Just as we arrived, Mom called from the house.

"Jerimy, Julie, I could use a little help."

Jerimy groaned. "I should have set the clock for earlier. We could have gone with Dad."

"I don't know, Jerimy. That house looks so good to me I would help clean it with a toothbrush—and be happy while I did it," I joked.

"I know what you mean." Grinning, Jerimy added, "But you might have made a cute bald girl. I'll bet the boys at school would have just loved it," he joked. "Besides, I could have gotten in the bathroom in the morning."

"Funny, funny," I laughed as we walked in the back door.

"What are you two in such a good mood about?" Mom asked.

Jerimy grinned. Ignoring the strange look Mom gave him, he said, "We were just saying how glad we are to help. We will call this our housecleaning cycle."

Mom shook her head as she handed us a bucket and the window cleaner. "I'm not even going to ask what that is all about," she said. "But I am certainly glad to know that you will enjoy washing the outside of all the windows. You can call it your window washing cycle."

47

6 Mr. Z Disappears

All the next week, Jerimy argued that we should return the clock to Mr. Z.

"It's a chance in a lifetime," I kept saying. "We can actually watch history as it happens. We just won't go to the future anymore."

"We could become history," Jerimy said sarcastically. "Think how Mom and Dad would have felt if we hadn't come back. What if the Director had caught us? Mom and Dad wouldn't even know what had happened to us."

"But Mr. Z must have given us the clock for some reason," I argued. "What if it is something important that we are supposed to do?"

"Then we can ask him when we return the clock," Jerimy insisted. "But if he did have a reason, it was probably a bad one. You heard what Mart said. Mr. Z was banished because he killed someone."

"If he wants us to do something bad, we will just say no," I said.

"What if he tricked us, and we did what he wanted without even knowing?"

I didn't have an answer for that one, but the argument went on for days. Finally, I agreed to return to the antique store and, at least, talk to Mr. Z.

"For someone who wants to be a scientist, you are not very daring," I sulked.

Jerimy looked hurt. "There is a difference between being daring and dumb," he said. "And messing around with something that we don't know anything about is dumb. I shouldn't have fixed the clock in the first place."

Jerimy and I could have saved all that arguing. When we returned to the store the next day after school, the shop was completely bare.

Jerimy pressed his nose against the dirty window. "It looks like it's been empty for years."

I cupped my hands around my eyes and peered inside the dark store. Only a few trails in the dust suggested anyone had ever been inside the dingy store. "I don't understand. Where could he have gone?" I asked.

"It just proves he was up to no good," Jerimy said. "I think he set that whole thing up to give us the clock. He knew that you liked antiques. Sooner or later you would have gone to his store."

"Let's ask at the bookstore next door," I suggested. "Maybe they know something."

Jerimy shrugged, as though he knew it was useless, but he followed me to the bookstore. The lady behind the counter had her mousy brown hair tied up neatly in a bun, and her glasses hung from a chain around her neck. She looked brisk and businesslike, not the type to bother answering questions from kids. But she looked up curiously when I asked about Mr. Z.

"That was the strangest thing," she mused. "That man moved all those boxes and clocks into the store and only stayed for a couple of days. I went to the store once. I thought it would be a friendly gesture—you know—to help him get started. He did have some marvelous antiques. But he wouldn't sell me anything. Said it was all his own private collection. Now why would a person open a shop to keep his collection of antiques, I ask you? Then two days later, he was gone. I came to work one morning, and the shop was empty. He never even bothered to clean it. It is very strange, I tell you."

Jerimy and I looked at each other. We had talked about Mr. Z picking us for the clock, but we had only half believed it. Now there could be no doubt. He had gone to a lot of trouble to make sure we got the clock. What kind of evil motives could he have had?

"I don't get it," Jerimy mumbled on the way home. We had thanked the clerk and left the bookstore still unable to think clearly. "What could he have wanted us to do? What could a kid do that a grown-up couldn't do better? Why didn't he give the clock to an adult? Maybe something happens because we have the clock—something beyond our control."

"I wonder if he still watches us," I asked as I nervously glanced around the quiet street.

"Who knows?" Jerimy said. "We've been so busy with the clock, we haven't been paying attention. If we were smart, we would throw it away, right now. We could pitch it in that trash can over there. Then we wouldn't have to worry."

"What if someone found it, like a criminal, for instance?" I asked.

"We could take a hammer and smash it up so it could never be fixed," Jerimy said. He shrugged his shoulders and added sadly, "But I guess I couldn't bring myself to do that. Gee, I wish I knew exactly how it worked."

"Look," I said, "we don't know for sure that Mr. Z is bad. Maybe we are to use the time clock for something good. If we destroy the clock, we will never find out." I took a deep breath. "Why don't we put the clock away and wait to see if anything happens?"

Jerimy nodded. "That's a good idea," he agreed. "I'd like to do some more time traveling, too. It would be a terrific experiment. But right now there is so much we don't know." He paused, then looked straight at me. "Agreed then. No more time travel until we find out what Mr. Z wants."

I had to admit he was right. "All right," I agreed. "Let's wait and see."

By the time we got home, dinner was ready. Mom had fixed spaghetti, my favorite food. But I couldn't eat. I was too excited thinking of all the wonderful things we could see with the time clock. Jerimy's appetite wasn't bothered, though. He ate two helpings and topped it off with a bowl of ice cream.

"Are you coming down with something?" Mom asked, feeling my head. "You hardly touched your dinner."

"I'm just not hungry," I shrugged. "I'm thinking about the story I have to write for an English assignment. I thought I might write about time travelers." Jerimy shot a startled look at me and kicked my leg. I ignored him. "Where would you go if you had a time machine?" I asked Mom.

"That's easy," Mom said dreamily. "I'd go back to the time of knights and fair maidens, when castles dotted the countryside."

Dad snorted. "Yes, to a time when a handsome knight would lock up his fair maiden in a drafty castle while he rode off to slay his enemy." He added with a grin, "People had fleas in those days, besides. Not too romantic, if you ask me."

Mom shuddered. We all know how she is about bugs. Seeing a spider nearly makes her faint. "Well, it's only pretend, anyway," she sighed. "I guess when you think about life in another time, it sometimes appears better than it actually was." Mom really is a romantic.

"Where would you go, Dad?" Jerimy asked, getting into the conversation.

"Let me see. I think I would go back and visit your

grandpa when he was a boy. He used to always tell me stories about how hard it was when he was young. He had to get up every morning and milk the cows and afterwards walk five miles to school."

"You say the same things," Mom said. "How many times have you reminded the kids how hard you worked when you were young?"

"It's the truth," Dad sniffed. "We lived on a dairy farm. I had to help with the milking twice a day. After each milking, all the equipment had to be scrubbed and sterilized. It was a lot of work. Kids today just don't know how easy they have it." Dad suddenly grinned. "I remember my dad saying those very same words to me because they didn't have milking machines when he was a boy, or a school bus to take him to school."

"Did you know Dad when he was young?" I asked Mom. The conversation was getting more interesting. Mom and Dad never talked about their lives as kids—except, of course, when Dad mentioned how much harder he had to work.

"I didn't move to Crystal Springs until I was twelve," Mom said. "Just about the age you are now. I met your dad right after that. His parents had just sold the farm and moved into town. He had to change schools, too. Being new in town gave us something in common, and we became friends. He was my sweetheart from then on." She smiled at Dad, and he winked back.

"Why did your parents sell the farm?" Jerimy asked. "I

think it would be kind of nice to live in the country."

"It's a long story," Dad said. "Your grandmother's health wasn't good, and she wanted to get away from all that work. Dad didn't want to leave, but one day the barn burned down, and they couldn't afford to rebuild it. After that, Mom finally convinced him to sell."

"How did the barn burn down?" I asked.

"Grandpa went to the barn one day to milk. I wasn't there because I was playing baseball. Our team was up for the championship. We won it, too." Across the table I heard Jerimy sigh, but Dad went on with his story and didn't notice.

"Anyway, Grandpa surprised an old bum who was sleeping in the barn. The bum ran out and locked the door. I suppose it was to give himself time to get away. Just then Dad discovered the barn was on fire. At first we thought the bum had set it, perhaps with the pipe we found afterwards. The fire marshal, however, determined that it was faulty wiring. Anyway, my father was locked in, and the only other way out was through the loft, which was blocked by flames."

"How did he get out?" I asked.

"A couple of kids came by on their bikes and heard his cries. They unlocked the door, and saved Dad's life. Dad managed to save all the animals, but the barn was a complete loss. We sure were grateful to those kids, but we never did discover who they were."

"That's a good story," I sighed, "but it doesn't really help me decide if time travel would be a good thing or not."

"Maybe it would depend on the people using it," Mom said. "In the story, *The Time Machine*, it was a good thing. The hero saved the human race."

"I think it is good that there isn't such a thing," Dad said. "You can't change what is meant to be. Time travel would open up a lot of strange possibilities, and it would also create a lot of problems."

This time it was Jerimy's turn to smirk. But part of what Dad said was true. Ever since Jerimy had fixed the clock, life had been nothing but problems. I almost wished I had never heard of Mr. Z or his stupid clock.

7 An Old-time Fourth of July

The time machine had filled all our days and thoughts, and neither Jerimy nor I had started on a project for the science fair at school. Now it was only two weeks away, and I hadn't even decided what I was going to do. It wasn't any problem for Jerimy, of course. He had a contraption with wire, lights, and gadgets coming to life in his room. He had offered to help me, but I wanted to try something on my own. But now I had to come up with an idea, and I was getting desperate.

That's why I was sitting at the kitchen table late one afternoon, surrounded by a stack of books I had checked out of the library. The house was quiet. Mom had taken Jerimy to the hardware store for something he needed for his project.

As I thumbed through my third book, suddenly, a shadow fell over the pages. Nervously, I glanced up. The sun would not set for several hours, and it seemed as bright as ever. But what had made the shadow? I wondered. Silly,

I scolded myself. The sun must have gone behind a cloud. I looked back at my book. There was a sound outside, a little snap, like a branch being broken. I froze, listening, but everything was deathly still. I tried to get back to my reading, but I couldn't concentrate. Mom had told me to lock the door when she left, but had I remembered to do it? I wasn't sure. I checked my watch. Mom and Jerimy had been gone half an hour. They should be coming back any minute, I thought with relief. Then a chill ran up my back. What if they couldn't find the part Jerimy needed and went to Crystal Springs' other hardware store? It was clear across town. Worse yet, what if someone were outside, waiting to grab them?

I pretended to read, but my mind was racing as I tried to decide what to do. Again, the shadow darkened the pages of my book. This time the shadow had a definite shape. Part of me didn't want to look up because I already knew what I would see. That didn't stop me from screaming, however, when I turned and saw that evil face pressed up against the window.

My scream must have startled Mr. Z. Perhaps he hadn't really meant for me to see him. At any rate, he stumbled backwards and disappeared from view. By the time I recovered and ran to the window, he was nowhere in sight. I checked both the front and the back doors. Locked. I had remembered after all.

When I calmed down, I thought about the situation. If I called the police, or even told Mom when she returned, I would have to explain about the time clock. One or two things would happen. First, and most likely, Mom would think I made the whole thing up. If she and Dad did believe me, however, they would make me turn the clock over to the authorities. Scientists and government people would whisk it away for study, and that would be the end of that.

What was Mr. Z doing? Could he have been trying to regain the clock? That didn't make sense. Whatever we were supposed to do, I was sure it hadn't been done yet. Was he only checking to see if we had fixed the clock? Maybe he thought everyone was gone. After all, the car was gone, and the house probably looked empty. In the end, I decided to say nothing.

My mind was still on the mysterious Mr. Z when, suddenly, the door rattled and swung open. I gasped with fright, but before I screamed again, Mom and Jerimy walked in.

"I didn't hear you drive up," I said, collapsing back in my chair.

"I'm sorry, honey," Mom said. "I didn't mean to give you a start. But I am glad you remembered to lock the doors."

Not half as glad as I am, I thought.

Jerimy looked at me oddly. He always knows when something is wrong. He didn't say anything until Mom had left the room.

"What happened?" he whispered.

"Mr. Z. He was here, looking through the window at me. We've got to find out what we are supposed to do with the clock," I insisted.

"If it was anything good, he would have told us and not spied on us," Jerimy said. "I would still like to take that clock apart," he added, "and really check it out. There is a little capsule-like thing inside that seems to give it power. I would like to find out what it is."

"You promised you would wait," I said.

"So did you," Jerimy reminded me.

I left the clock at the back of the closet for a whole week. But it kept eating at me whenever I thought of all the things I could see. Even so, I might not have tried to use it again if Mom and Dad had not gone out the following Saturday night.

They were going out to dinner and a movie, and they called Mrs. Murphy to baby-sit. Jerimy and I would be unhappy about having a baby-sitter, except that we both love Mrs. Murphy. She used to take care of Mom when she was young. We met her right after we moved back. Mom says Mrs. Murphy enjoys the company, and it makes her feel useful. She is really sweet, but she always falls asleep in the chair in front of the TV.

Jerimy went to his room right after dinner to finish his science project. I talked with Mrs. Murphy, and we played a couple of games. By eight-thirty she was dozing in the chair, and I was bored watching TV by myself. I wandered upstairs and got the time clock. I sat on the bed looking at it.

Suddenly, Jerimy burst into the room. "I thought so," he said. His voice was louder than it needed to be. "You promised you would wait."

"I wasn't going without you," I sighed. "Honest. I was just sitting here thinking. How many people get a chance like this? And here we are just letting it go to waste. There are so many things we could learn."

Jerimy sat down on the bed beside me. "You know, when we first used the time clock, it was just a scientific experiment for me. I was only curious about how the clock operated and what we would find. I didn't care about the people—until we met Mart. Now I feel different. It gives you kind of a nice feeling to have a friend, even if you never see him again. Do you understand?"

I nodded. "The silly thing is that now I am wondering about other people," he said sheepishly, "the people who settled this town, for instance. What were they like, do you suppose? You know, if we went back you could get a real antique, one that really meant something to you. It's your clock, really, and I guess I don't have the right to stop you, if you want to use it. That's why I came to your room, to tell you that."

"You're a pretty good brother," I said, giving him a kiss on the cheek, which made him squirm with embarrassment.

"We still have to be careful," he warned.

I nodded. "Let me check on Mrs. Murphy. Then we'll have to find something to wear. Remember what happened in the future."

I tiptoed downstairs and peeked at Mrs. Murphy. She hadn't moved, and I could hear her soft snores over the sound of the TV. Satisfied, I hurried back up and searched through my closet.

Last year the American school had put on a play about pioneers, and I had a part. Mom had made my costume, a calico dress and matching bonnet. It was probably a little short by now, but it would do. Feeling a little silly, I pulled the dress over my jeans.

I looked in the mirror. What a lot of bother it must have been to be a girl in the old days. You always had to wear a bonnet because it wasn't ladylike to have a suntan. Girls were supposed to be pale and delicate, even if they weren't.

Jerimy was ready when I got back to his room. He had on an old flannel shirt and a straw hat.

"You look like Huckleberry Finn," I giggled.

He looked at me critically. "You look like that girl in 'Little House on the Prairie.'"

"Maybe we'll look like we belong, then," I said. "Come on, before Mrs. Murphy wakes up."

We crept down the stairs, carefully avoiding the third step from the bottom. That's the one that always creaks, and I didn't want to have to explain to Mrs. Murphy why we were creeping out of the house, dressed like we were going to a Halloween party. We slipped past the living room door and into the kitchen. A minute later we were out in the cold night air. With a sigh of relief, I pulled the kitchen door closed.

"I have a terrific idea," Jerimy said. "Let me pick the time, OK?"

"Make sure it is summer," I shivered.

I wished I had brought a sweater. October nights get cold in Crystal Springs. Frosty leaves crunched under my feet as we walked back to the boxes.

"How about a hundred years ago?" Jerimy suggested. "We could get a good feel of what it was like, and it wouldn't be so wild that we would get into trouble."

"Anytime, just so it's warm," I said as I sat down beside him.

It was summer all right. I think Jerimy must have picked the hottest day of the year. The heat hit us like a blast from a furnace after the cool night we had been in a few seconds before. We were in a thick patch of woods, but even there we could not escape from the heat.

From somewhere nearby, we could hear horses. Wagon wheels creaked and groaned down a bumpy road. Dust flew up in the air, only to settle back down on everything.

"The road is about the same place it is now," Jerimy said, pointing through the woods. "But our house won't be built for about ninety years." He stuck the clock inside his shirt and led the way through the bushes that bordered the road.

Crouching behind some trees at the edge of the road, we watched. Some buggies passed, and so did a few riders on horseback. Everyone seemed headed for town.

"I wonder what is going on?" I asked. "Why would so many people be going to town?"

"It's the Fourth of July," Jerimy grinned. "I figured everyone would be going to town to celebrate. No one will even notice us with all the excitement. If they do, we can say we just moved here."

I gave him an admiring glance. "Good thinking."

Pushing aside the dust-covered branches, we took advantage of a short break in traffic to climb out on the road. A few minutes later, as we trudged along in the heat, I heard the clop, clop of a horse behind us. We moved over to let a wagon pass.

"It's a mighty long walk to town on such a hot day," a kindly voice boomed out beside us. It was the driver of a brightly polished wagon pulled by two sleek horses.

He was a huge man with a handlebar mustache and friendly brown eyes. A wide-brimmed, gray felt hat shaded his eyes from the sun, and he looked hot and uncomfortable in his Sunday suit. I had a feeling he was much more used to work clothes. Beside him a plump motherly woman held a baby on her lap.

"Where are your folks?" the man asked.

"They will be coming along soon, sir," Jerimy answered politely. "They still had some chores to do, but they said we could come ahead."

"Can't wait for all the excitement, hey?" the man chuckled. "I believe I would be looking forward to the festivities a mite more if it wasn't so darn hot."

Sweating beneath my jeans and long dress, I nodded in agreement. "It is awfully hot," I said.

"Don't think I have seen you two before. Are your folks new to Crystal Springs?"

Jerimy pointed back to the woods where a hundred years later our house would stand. "We just moved here, yes, sir."

"Why, I'll bet your folks bought the Tittleman farm. That means we'll be neighbors. I'm John Weatherby. We live on the next farm down the road. Hop in the back, and we'll give you a ride into town."

There didn't seem to be a polite way to refuse, and in this heat a ride did sound good. We jumped in the back as the wagon started again on its bumpy way.

"Hello." For the first time I noticed a small blond girl nearly hidden by a bale of straw. "My name is Eliza Jane. I heard you telling Pa you just moved in. I'm so glad. Maybe we will be friends."

I gulped and nodded. "My name is Julie, and this is Jerimy. He's my twin brother."

"Julie," she repeated. "I like that name. I've never met any twins before. It will be nice to have neighbors my age. I'm eleven, twelve next month."

"That's how old we are," I said when I could get in a word. I felt guilty for getting up her hopes, though. I couldn't help but wonder what she would think when she found out that we really weren't neighbors.

Eliza Jane smiled. "It's going to be so much fun today, don't you think? Pa says there will be a band, and the whole town is having a picnic. In the afternoon, there will be horse races."

"It sounds like fun," I agreed.

Jerimy had been staring at her with fascination. "Will there be any gunmen in town, do you think?"

I gave him a warning look, but he ignored me. Eliza Jane looked puzzled. "Gunmen?"

"You know, outlaws, desperados," Jerimy explained eagerly.

"I certainly hope not," Eliza Jane said primly. "But there will be a sharpshooting contest," she added. "Pa usually wins that.

"Mr. Tate is Pa's only real competition, when he's not drinking." She giggled. "Old Mr. Tate gets drunk sometimes. He used to shoot up the sign over the livery stable." She glanced at her parents. "I'm not supposed to know about things like that, but one of the boys at school told me. He says Mr. Tate did it to have a place to sleep. The sheriff locked him up almost every night, especially when it was cold. Finally, the mayor complained. He said the town shouldn't have to pay to keep Mr. Tate all winter."

"So what happened?" I asked.

"Mr. Tate said the mayor was so fat he would make a better target than the sign," Eliza Jane giggled. "After that the mayor didn't say another word. The sheriff made a deal with Mr. Tate. If he would stop shooting up the town, he could still stay in the jail. I think he made Mr. Tate a janitor to make it official."

Jerimy and I laughed at her story. I leaned back against the straw and smiled contentedly. This was going to be even more fun with a friend to share it with. Then I had a sad thought. Eliza Jane would be dead by now. If not, she would be one hundred and eleven years old. Even Grandpa had not yet been born, and no matter how much I wanted to be friends, it just could not be. Eliza Jane belonged to the past we call history, and Jerimy and I belonged to another world called the future.

8 A Friend
and a Foe

Even before we reached the town square, I could feel the
excitement in the air. Little tables were set up in the park,
and the women bustled about getting things ready for the
picnic. The men, looking uncomfortable and stiff in their
good clothes, stood about in small groups discussing crops
and betting on the horses for the races later in the day. On
one corner, a brass band enthusiastically played marching
music, adding to the noise and good spirits of the crowd.

Mr. Weatherby tied his horses to a ring set in a stone
post in front of the bank. The bank was a small unpainted
building, like most of the others, although the courthouse
and a few other buildings were brick. A church made from
red bricks caught my attention. It looked very familiar,
and after staring at it for awhile, I remembered seeing the
same church in downtown Crystal Springs. It had changed
very little in a hundred years, but, among the wooden
structures, it was even more noticeable now.

The town was bigger than I expected. Wooden sidewalks

ran on both sides of Main Street, and they were crowded with people walking or visiting with friends. I could tell that Independence Day was an important occasion for the town. There were probably few occasions to have a holiday, and everyone was making the most of this one.

Jerimy's eyes darted about as he tried to see everything at once. "This is terrific," he grinned when he caught my eye.

I nodded. He had probably picked the best day of all to understand the past. Perhaps it was because the United States was newer, but these people were really celebrating our country's independence.

A second later, a wave of panic swept over me. A man ducked around the corner of the stable. I only had a quick glimpse, but I thought I recognized Mr. Z. I started to tell Jerimy, but by that time the man returned. He was not Mr. Z, after all. I breathed a sigh of relief but, from that moment, some of the glow was lost. The puzzle of Mr. Z hung like a shadow over everything I did.

"Was that someone you knew?" Eliza Jane asked.

"I thought so. Someone from where we used to live," I said. "But it wasn't, after all."

"Where did you live before?" Eliza Jane asked.

"New York," I said, naming the first city that came into my head.

"Chicago," Jerimy answered in the same breath. He spoke quickly to cover our mistake. "First we lived in New York, then Chicago."

"You are lucky," Eliza Jane sighed. "I've never been anywhere but here."

"You young people can walk around for a while." Mr. Weatherby's suggestion saved us from further questions. "Just don't get yourselves in trouble. And bring your parents over when they arrive. I would like to meet them," he shouted after us.

I looked anxiously at Jerimy, but he shrugged. "We'll be gone before they get suspicious," he whispered.

"What would you like to do first?" Eliza Jane asked.

"Let's just walk around and look at everything," Jerimy suggested. We crossed the street, stopping to watch some boys throwing firecrackers. At every explosion, the horses rolled their eyes and pranced nervously.

"Those boys go to school with me," Eliza Jane said, "but they are very rowdy. We had better get away."

The warning came too late. The oldest boy in the group caught sight of us and blocked our way. He was a big boy, with flaming red hair and bare feet. He jammed his hands down in the pockets of his faded dungarees and looked us over scornfully.

"Who're your friends, Eliza Jane?" he sneered.

"None of your business, George," Eliza Jane said. "Now you let us pass, or I'll tell your father."

"Looks like a sissy to me," George challenged Jerimy. He slowly circled him, his eyes glaring as he looked Jerimy up and down. It was plain to see George wanted a fight.

Jerimy's ears turned red, but he answered calmly, "I'm

69

Jerimy, and this is my sister, Julie."

"Where did you get those funny shoes?" George asked mockingly.

Too late I remembered our tennis shoes. I didn't know when they had been invented, but I knew it wasn't that long ago. I scuffled my feet, trying to hide my shoes under a too-short dress.

"She has them on, too," one of the other boys hooted. "They must be girls' shoes. We have two new girls in town."

Jerimy tried to brush past George, but George wasn't about to stop now. He pushed him back with one hand. Jerimy's voice dropped to a deadly low. "I was told this town was full of country boys too dumb to do anything but pull a plow. I see that's true."

It was hard to tell from where I stood just who threw the first punch. One minute they stood on the corner, having a glaring match, and the next they were rolling on the ground. All I could see were elbows and knees amid a ball of dust. On the first roll, the time clock slipped out of Jerimy's shirt. I made a grab for it, but one of the boys pushed me back and held my arms. Another boy held a sputtering and kicking Eliza Jane.

"The clock," I shouted. "Don't break it."

Jerimy grabbed the clock, but his move gave George an opening. With a sickening thud, a punch landed in Jerimy's eye. The boy holding me reached for the clock, pulling me along. When he had the clock in his free hand, he held it teasingly above his head.

"Hey, hey. What's all this?" Mr. Weatherby appeared out of nowhere. He grabbed the two fighters by the scruffs of their necks, holding them apart easily. "Fighting," he scolded. "What would your parents think?"

"He started it," George whined.

"That's a lie, George." Eliza Jane put her hands on her hips. "Now give them back their clock."

"Did you take something of theirs?" Mr. Weatherby asked sternly.

The boy who held the clock gave it back, but his look clearly said this was not the end. The three boys took off down the street.

"Doesn't look to me like you made any friends there," Mr. Weatherby winked. "But perhaps they will think a second time when you see them again. That was a pretty good scrap, from what I saw."

"I guess it's over, at least for now," Jerimy said with a painful grin.

"I hope for your sake that's true," Mr. Weatherby smiled. "You already have one shiner."

Jerimy gingerly touched his eye, and winced. "Great. How am I going to explain this to Mom and Dad?"

Mr. Weatherby chuckled. "I imagine your folks know boys sometimes fight. Don't think too harshly of George. He's really not such a bad sort. His mother died not long ago, and his pa is so wrapped up in grieving, he has forgotten about the boy. But George will be all right, given a little time."

"Did you break the clock?" I asked when Mr. Weatherby had gone.

Jerimy looked it over carefully. "It looks OK, but I can't really tell."

"What kind of a clock is that?" Eliza Jane asked. "I've never seen one like that."

"It's a family heirloom," I lied. I could tell she still thought it peculiar, but she was too polite to ask further. I didn't like to lie to Eliza Jane, but what choice did I have? Even if we told her the truth, she would never believe it.

I could see she was curious about the tennis shoes, too. She peeked at them every so often when she thought I wasn't looking. Another lie.

"They are a new kind," I said. "Everyone in Chicago is wearing them."

"They look terribly comfortable," she said wistfully, "but Pa would never let me wear them."

"It might be a while before shoes like that show up here," Jerimy mumbled. His eye was already turning an ugly black.

"Let's look around some more," I suggested, trying to change the subject.

The next few hours went by all too fast. There were lots of games, including sack races and catching a greased pig. Jerimy almost won that one, but the pig wriggled away at the last minute and was caught by another boy. It was just as well. The first prize was the pig, which might have been hard to explain to our parents.

"You have some talents I didn't know about," I teased when Jerimy and I had a minute alone. "I hope one of them is making up stories because we are going to need one for that eye."

"I'll think of something," Jerimy promised.

"You two are so different from anyone I've ever met," Eliza Jane said later as we sat eating lunch on the town square. Our plates were piled high with chicken, fresh baked ham, and heavenly pies and cakes. Jerimy and I had decided that we could not stay much longer. Mr. Weatherby had already asked several times about our parents. We had tried to convince him that chores might have prevented them from coming, but several times I had noticed him staring at us. Did he suspect that we weren't telling the truth? I wondered.

"Why do you say we are different?" Jerimy asked.

"I can't really explain it," Eliza Jane said. "But I really like both of you. I hope we will become close friends."

I looked at her sadly. "We really like it here, too. But I don't think we will be staying."

"But why not?" Eliza Jane asked. "You just moved here."

I hesitated, wondering what would happen if I told her who we really were. Suddenly, I saw someone duck behind the corner of a building. I grabbed Jerimy's arm.

"I just saw George and his friends trying to sneak up on us," I said. "They might be after the time clock, and I don't think you are in any shape to fight them again. We'd better get out of here."

"We can't just disappear in the middle of town," Jerimy protested.

"We can duck in that alley," I said. Jerimy nodded and grabbed my hand. We darted down the street.

Not knowing what was happening, Eliza Jane ran behind us. When we reached the alley, Jerimy stopped so suddenly I almost tripped over him. There, blocking the alley, stood George, grinning smugly. Out of the corner of my eye I saw one of the other boys come up behind us, cutting off our escape. We had run right into a trap.

"Well, well," George smiled. "Fancy meeting up with you again. The sissy with the clock. Hand it over. I want to see what makes it so special."

Jerimy reached in his shirt, as though he was going to hand the clock to George. I squeezed my eyes shut and crossed my fingers. Had the clock been damaged in the scuffle earlier in the day? When I opened my eyes, I discovered an even worse worry. As Jerimy yanked the pin on the clock, setting us in motion, George made a lunge for it. He touched Jerimy, just as Eliza Jane, trying to help, grabbed for George. We headed back to our own time, but this time we took along two unsuspecting guests.

9 A Surprising Discovery

Eliza Jane's eyes filled with fear. "What happened? Where are we?"

George was still crouched, reaching for the time clock. He stood up slowly, staring in amazement as a semi passed us on the road. The blood drained from his face, leaving his freckles brighter than ever. "What is going on?" he demanded, trying to hide his fear.

Jerimy groaned. "I knew it. I knew something like this was going to happen."

Eliza Jane took my arm. "Please tell me what is happening. What is this place? How did we get here?"

"We didn't die, did we?" George asked, pinching himself to make sure.

I sighed. "You are never going to believe this, but you are still on the square. It's a little bigger than it was in your day, but it's the same square. The alley by the livery stable where we were standing is part of it now. Look, don't you recognize the fountain?"

Eliza Jane and George looked at the fountain. "I guess it does look the same. But it couldn't be, could it?" Eliza Jane asked weakly.

Jerimy touched her arm. "Don't be afraid. We'll take you back. But I guess we owe you an explanation."

"It's that clock!" George exclaimed. "You did it with the clock. That's why it's so important. That's why you seem different." He was smarter than we thought.

Eliza Jane was calmer now, more so than I would have been in her place. She still flinched every time a car passed, but her voice was steady. She walked over to a park bench and sat down. "Tell me about all this," she said.

We managed to explain the clock. I wasn't sure she was convinced, but now she seemed more curious than afraid.

George was, too. He seemed fascinated by the cars on the street. "Those must be terrific," he said. "They go so fast. Do you suppose I could ride in one?"

"I wish we could show you more," Jerimy said, "but the longer you are here, the more chance you have of getting caught. You must promise not to tell anyone." He added, with a grin, "Not that anyone would believe you. But promise, just in case."

Eliza Jane giggled. "They would think we had been out in the sun too long if we told. You must be awfully brave."

Jerimy and I squirmed uncomfortably. "Wait," Jerimy shouted. "I know something you might want to try." He dashed across the street. A second later he was back with a can of pop from the machine at the laundromat.

"I love it," Eliza Jane said, wrinkling her nose at the bubbles. She sighed, "I suppose it's one of those things I'll have to wait for. Like those funny-looking shoes."

"And that funny fastener," George said, pointing to Jerimy's zipper.

"That's called a zipper," I said. "I think it gets invented pretty soon. Maybe you would like to see what girls wear now," I said, slipping the dress over my head.

Eliza Jane stared, and George looked shocked. "You wear pants like a boy? All the time? Even to school?" George growled. When I nodded, he shook his head. "I don't think I would like that. Girls are supposed to wear dresses."

"I do once in a while," I said, "but they are short." I couldn't resist adding, "About up to here," to see the horrified look on George's face as I pointed to my knees. We shared the rest of the pop in silence.

"Will I ever see you again?" Eliza Jane asked, finally.

I shook my head. "If we keep going back, somone is sure to wonder."

"I would like to stay here," George said, still watching the cars.

Jerimy looked nervous. "No, you wouldn't. Your life is there."

George stared at him for a second. "I guess," he said, shrugging his shoulders. He looked at Jerimy's eye. "I'm sorry about the fight," he added.

"Me, too," Jerimy said.

"I'd like to know. . .no, maybe I wouldn't like to know what my life is going to be," Eliza Jane said. "But you know what would be nice? For you to come back and visit me later in my life. I'll never forget you, not in my whole life. We've only known each other a few hours, but it's as if we've been friends forever."

"In a way, I guess that's true," Jerimy tried to joke. "Maybe we could come back—if we can find you."

"We had better go back now," Jerimy said. "Just hold on to us," he ordered as we walked back to the spot where we had changed time.

George suddenly laughed. "If Pete and John are still in the alley, I can't wait to see the looks on their faces."

"Don't tell them what happened," Jerimy warned.

"Oh, I won't," George promised. "I'll just let them think they've gone daft," he grinned.

The alley, however, was deserted when we returned. Eliza Jane and George stood silently while Jerimy reset the time. Eliza Jane took my hands and gave them a squeeze. "I won't forget you."

"We won't forget you, either," Jerimy said. To my surprise, there was sadness in his eyes.

Back in our own time, I picked up the dress from under the park bench where I had left it. We were nearly a mile away from home. Walking quickly and staying in the bushes to avoid being seen, we started back. Jerimy was unusually quiet.

"I guess we lost your time machine boxes," I said. "Maybe we can make another, although we don't really seem to need it."

Jerimy still didn't talk. "It seems odd to think that Eliza Jane is dead now, doesn't it?" I said, trying to make him talk.

"You are the one who is always telling me to get out with people more," Jerimy said bitterly. "Well, I did, and look what's happened. I have a black eye and a friend who is dead before I was even born. At least my test tubes and experiments don't make me feel bad."

I thought about that for a while. "No, they don't, I suppose. But then, they don't make you feel good, either. You don't give people a chance. Sure there are going to be some who think you are weird, but if you would let people know you, most would like you. Like me. I like you."

"Sisters don't count."

"How about Eliza Jane? She liked you. Just think of her as living in a different place. That's what I'm going to do."

Jerimy didn't answer, but I could tell by the look on his face that he was thinking about what I said as we hurried up the drive to our house. I peeked in the living room window. "Mrs. Murphy is still asleep," I reported with relief. "Now, if we can just think of a good story for your eye." I paused. A figure lurking at the end of the drive caught my eye.

Jerimy saw it, too. "It's Mr. Z. There. By the bushes. I'm going to find out what is going on."

Before I could protest, he was gone. I debated what I should do. Should I follow, or stay back in case I needed to get help? The only sound was a dog barking somewhere up the street. The night seemed to have simply swallowed them up. Finally, I saw Jerimy's outline at the end of the drive. Although there was no sign of Mr. Z, I couldn't stop shaking. Had he really gone, or was he somewhere in the dark, watching our every move?

Jerimy came back up the drive. "Gone," he reported disappointedly. "Why won't he face us and explain what he wants?" He kicked at some rocks in disgust.

"Let's forget it. I'm freezing," I said, not wanting Jerimy to know how scared I felt.

We slipped back in through the kitchen door. A check on Mrs. Murphy showed her to be still sound asleep.

"How does my eye look?" Jerimy asked.

"It's bad. We'd better put some ice on it. I don't know what we are going to tell Mom and Dad."

Jerimy grinned. "I'll say we had an argument, and you punched me."

"Don't you dare," I said.

"I'll think of something," Jerimy promised as he went to his room. I went to my own room and hung up the dress— just in time. I heard Mom and Dad walk in the door and thank Mrs. Murphy.

"They were perfect angels, as usual," Mrs. Murphy reported cheerfully. "They were so quiet I hardly knew they were here."

As soon as Dad left to drive Mrs. Murphy home, Mom came upstairs. "What happened to your eye?" she cried the minute she saw Jerimy.

"I tripped," Jerimy said. Then he grinned. "Actually, I found this time clock that can take you anywhere you want to go. I went back in time about a hundred years, just to see what it was like. I met this bully named George, who turned out not so bad after all, but at first he tried to take the time clock, and we had a terrific fight. But, as you can see, I managed to save the time clock and make it back in one piece, or, at least, almost one piece."

Mom was very quiet through all this, and I held my breath. What on earth was Jerimy thinking of? Mom stood with her hand on her hip, staring at Jerimy. Suddenly, she broke into a laugh and shook her head.

"That must be the tallest tale any parent was ever told." She was still chuckling as she made an ice pack. "What did you trip over?" she asked. Her eyes lit on the string Jerimy had running from his bed to the light switch, which allowed him to turn off the light when he was in bed. "I'll bet I can guess what you tripped over," Mom said.

"Sometimes I forget the string is there," Jerimy said.

Mom sighed deeply. "This room isn't fit for human habitation. You are simply going to have to get rid of about half of this junk, before you break your neck."

"Junk?" Jerimy looked indignant. "I need all this stuff."

"Nevertheless, I want it cleaned up before the health department closes us down."

"I will," Jerimy promised.

"First thing in the morning," Mom said firmly.

"First thing in the morning," Jerimy agreed unhappily.

"I'll help you," I offered.

"Good," Mom nodded. "I think he's going to need all the help he can get."

"By the way," I asked as casually as I could, "if you wanted to find out something about someone who lived in a town a long time ago, what would you do? Just a regular person, not someone famous."

"Well, you might look through old newspapers and records in the library," Mom said. "If it's someone from this town that you're interested in, your best bet would be Grandpa Fenton. He collected so much information while researching our family that he's going to compile a history of the county. You know your father's family was one of the first to settle here."

"I didn't know that," Jerimy replied.

"It's true," Mom said. "Your great-great-great-great-grandfather Weatherby's family moved here well over a hundred years ago and started the farm."

I gulped. "Did you say Weatherby?" I saw the same shocked look on Jerimy's face, but Mom didn't notice.

She nodded. "His daughter, Eliza Jane, married a shop-keeper named Fenton. One of their sons moved back to the farm. That's the same farm where your dad was born."

"I would like to find out more," I said when I regained my voice. No wonder we had felt that special closeness to

Eliza Jane. She was our great-great-great-grandmother. Now more than ever, I wanted to find her and visit her once more. I thought of her sweet face and twinkling eyes and knew she would enjoy the joke as much as we did. I could hardly wait to tell her.

10 *Unwelcome Visitors*

Jerimy and I planned to go to Grandpa's house right after church Sunday morning, but we didn't get the chance. As soon as we arrived home from church, Mom told us not to change our clothes.

"I've invited the Johnsons for dinner," she said.

Jerimy and I groaned. As I said before, one of the great things about being twins is that you always have company. But Mom reads a lot of books about being a good parent for twins. The latest one said she should encourage us to develop separate interests. Now if you asked me, I'd say that our interests are pretty far apart. But Mom says we spend too much time together, and we need to have other friends. She even tries to find friends for us. She invites people to our home who have kids our age. That might be a good idea because there are not any kids in the neighborhood, and it's hard to make friends when you are the new kids in school. There is only one problem. Sometimes the arrangement does not work out well. Like this time.

Marcy Johnson is twelve. She wears gold hoop earrings and purple nail polish and talks about nothing but boys. Her brother Tom is a year younger. He does nothing but read comic books the whole time he's here. Marcy talks constantly, but Tom hardly speaks, unless it is to argue with Marcy.

"Do we have to stay with them all day?" I groaned when Mom told us. "The last time Marcy was here she spent an hour telling me how to fix my hair."

"They are our guests," Mom said. "I expect you to make them feel welcome. I'm sure Marcy means well."

Jerimy and I went upstairs to wait. "Maybe they will have a flat tire and won't make it," I sighed.

Jerimy flopped down on his bed. "We would never be that lucky." He looked around his room and shook his head. "Look at this room. It's empty."

"At least you can walk without breaking a leg," I said. The night before, we had carried box after box of wires, batteries, and odds and ends out to the garage. If I knew Jerimy, he would have it all back in his room in a week.

"It's not so bad for you when Marcy and Tom come," I sighed. "At least you don't have to listen to Tom. You can just work on your experiments. I suppose all afternoon I'll have to listen to Marcy telling me what kind of clothes I should wear."

"Why don't you just tell her you're not interested? Maybe she really does think you are interested," Jerimy said.

"I don't want to hurt her feelings," I said, "but I wish I

could think of some way to keep her busy so I wouldn't have to listen."

Jerimy looked thoughtful. Just then the doorbell rang, and he sighed, "So much for flat tires."

"The kids are upstairs," we heard Mom say. "Go on up. I know they will be glad to see you."

Marcy breezed into the room and plopped on Jerimy's bed. Tom sat down in the corner and pulled out a stack of comic books from under his coat. Without a word, he started to read.

"How do you like my new nail polish?" Marcy asked. She waved ten almost black fingernails under my nose.

"Nice," I muttered politely.

"It makes her look like she's dead," Tom said, without looking up.

"You would think so. You are too dumb to recognize fashion when you see it," Marcy sneered. "His idea of fashion is a bathing suit with stars."

"I may not know fashion, but I know dead," Tom said mildly.

Marcy ignored him. She turned to me. "Do you have any makeup? I could teach you how to put it on."

"Don't do it, Julie," Tom said, finally looking up from his comic. "She will make you look as ugly as she is."

With an angry look, Marcy started to answer, but Jerimy interrupted.

"Cut it out, you two. Listen, how would you like to have some fun?"

"I played spin the bottle at a party the other day," Marcy said. "It was fun."

Tom made a throwing up sound.

"My idea is more fun than that, but you have to swear you won't tell anyone," Jerimy replied. His serious tone aroused my curiosity.

Even Tom looked interested. I wondered what Jerimy had planned. Surely he didn't intend to tell about the clock.

"I promise," Marcy said eagerly.

Tom nodded. "Me, too."

"We have to go outside so our parents can't see," Jerimy said mysteriously.

Tom started to pick up his comics, but Jerimy stopped him. "You won't need those." Tom sighed, but he put the comics down on the desk.

I let Marcy and Tom take the lead going outside and fell back to talk to Jerimy. "What's up? What are you doing?"

"We are just going to have a little fun," he grinned. He patted his shirt. The time clock!

"You can't tell them, of all people," I protested.

"I'm not. Just play along with me, OK?"

"OK," I agreed doubtfully.

"This had better be good," Marcy said, rubbing her hands. "It's cold out here."

"It will be," Jerimy grinned. "Julie has learned to hyp-notize people."

"Oh, sure," Marcy scoffed. "I'm supposed to believe that?"

"It's true," Jerimy insisted. "She's really good at it. She has learned how to make you think you are in a different place—say, for instance, 1,000,000 B.C.—right in the middle of an ice age."

Tom started to look interested. "Can you really?"

"She can't," Marcy sneered, "and even if she could, that sounds dumb. No one in their right mind would even want to go to 1,000,000 B.C.."

"No, it's lots of fun," I said, getting warmed up to the idea. "It's like being in a movie. Sit down, and I'll show you."

Still looking skeptical, Marcy sat on the ground next to me. Tom sat next to her, and Jerimy sat on the other side of me to make a circle.

"Hold hands," I said, making my voice sound mysterious. Marcy made a face, but she held Tom's hand without a protest.

"Oh, Spirits of the Underworld, help us pass through to times long past," I chanted.

"Hey, I thought you were going to hypnotize us," Tom protested. "This sounds like a séance."

"This is how I do it," I said sternly. "But you must concentrate."

Jerimy gave me an approving nod as his hand crept inside his shirt.

"This had better be good," Marcy said crossly.

"Close your eyes," I whispered. "Think of a world made of ice. Think of another time. Hold on tightly to the person next to you, and keep your eyes closed as we travel through time."

The familiar dizziness started. I felt Marcy's hand tighten on mine.

"Wow," Tom shouted, opening his eyes. "You really did it. It's almost like we are in another world."

"It's really all in your head," I said. "That's what they call the power of suggestion."

"I don't like it," Marcy whined. "I'm cold. Wake me up."

We sat on an empty stretch of dry, cold earth. The world around us was deathly quiet except for a whisper of wind swirling through the few twisted bushes, which struggled for existence.

"Don't wake us up yet," Tom protested. "I think it's fantastic. How did you do it? I didn't even feel you hypnotize me at all."

"It took a lot of practice," I said, trying to be serious. "An old native woman taught me the ancient secrets when I was very young."

"I'd like to look around a little," Jerimy said.

"Why? It's not even real," Marcy grumbled. "The least you could have done was make it warm."

Ignoring Marcy's grumbling, Jerimy walked to a small rise in the barren land where he bent to examine some mosses. Suddenly he froze. I saw him fumble frantically in his shirt for the clock and back up quickly towards us. "Julie, we have to go back now!" he whispered.

89

At that moment, I saw the reason for his panic lumber towards us, and wanted to scream. Marcy's face was a pasty white as she pointed to a huge shaggy bear heading straight for us. Amazingly, Marcy began to laugh.

"That's really good, Julie. A cave bear. He looks almost real. For a second you had me really scared."

The bear seemed almost as surprised to see us as we were to see him. He paused, rose up on his hind legs, and sniffed the air—probably wondering if we would make a good snack. Jerimy stumbled back into the circle, dropping the clock in his excitement. I grabbed it up just as Jerimy reached for Marcy and Tom. I didn't bother to set the clock. I just spun the hands and pulled the pin. The world of ice faded as the bear let out a mighty roar and charged toward us.

"This is more like it," Marcy exclaimed. Evidently, neither Marcy nor Tom had noticed the clock in their excitement. I sat on a fallen log, waiting for my knees to stop knocking. Jerimy sat beside me, pale and shaking, but Tom and Marcy were already exploring. They would never know how close Mr. and Mrs. Johnson came to being childless.

"At least it's warm," Jerimy said. "When is it?"

I peeked at the clock. "1650," I answered, handing it back to Jerimy to hide.

We were in a deep forest with lacy ferns and berry bushes curling around towering trees. Marcy was already picking juicy ripe berries and stuffing them in her mouth.

"I can almost taste these," she said with a contented sigh. "Ummm."

"We'd better not stay here very long," I told Jerimy. "What if there are Indians—or wild animals?"

"Indians?" Tom repeated. "You could let us have an adventure. We could meet some Indians," he said, the excitement rising in his voice.

Tom might have been a freak from the way Marcy looked at him. "You are so dumb. None of this is real. Remember?"

"Even you said it seemed real," Tom replied. "Julie could make us think we were having an adventure. Right?"

"Dumb," Marcy muttered again.

I fumbled for an excuse. "I don't think I can," I said. "It takes a lot of energy, and I am pretty tired."

I had wandered over to a thicket to try some of the berries myself. In a tree over my head, a bird screeched an alarm. The rest of the forest seemed peaceful and quiet. Sunlight streamed through the trees, casting leafy shadows on the ground. It was the same forest we had seen in Eliza Jane's time, yet here it was different. This one was untouched, unspoiled. It would not be for much longer, I thought sadly. In a few more centuries, people would begin to chop and clear. Eventually, our little house would stand on this spot, and much later a great city, where the people allowed their freedom to be stolen by robots, would take its place.

Jerimy must have understood my thoughts. He stood beside me. "It's beautiful, isn't it?"

I nodded, and he sighed. "We'd better go back. If we were attacked by Indians, Marcy and Tom wouldn't know enough to run. If they were hurt, it would be all my fault."

"I have to wake you up," I told Marcy and Tom. "Mom will be calling us for dinner."

They grumbled, but took their places as I directed.

"Ready," Jerimy mumbled.

"Close your eyes," I said, keeping up the pretense. "The Spirits of the Underworld will now guide us home to our own time and place."

"That was fun," Tom said, opening his eyes. "I wish you would have made some cave people or Indians, but that bear was really great."

I gave him a sickly smile. "Well, it was just a game, but don't forget to keep it a secret."

Even Marcy looked impressed. "I wish I could do something like that. I would be really popular if I could," she added wistfully. She looked at her watch in surprise. "That's weird. I could swear we had been hypnotized for hours. But my watch says only ten minutes have gone by."

11 A Visit with an Old Friend

"Hypnosis must be like dreaming," Jerimy suggested. "You know, a dream seems to last for a long time, but, actually, it's only a few minutes long."

That explanation seemed to satisfy Marcy. She stood up and brushed herself off. "Hey. There is something funny here. If everything we did was all in my mind, why are there berry stains on my hands?"

Tom checked his hands. "Mine, too," he said.

"I gave you the berries—like a prop—to add to the reality," I said quickly. "You really did eat them."

Luckily, Mom called us for dinner, and we didn't have to answer any more questions. She beamed at us as we trooped past. "I'm so glad to see you getting along. I knew you would if you just gave it a chance."

Mom had fried chicken for dinner, and the Johnsons had brought potato salad and baked beans to go with it. There wasn't enough room at the table for everyone, so Marcy, Tom, Jerimy, and I filled up our plates and ate on the living room floor, picnic style. Doing something together had, at least for a while, brought Marcy and Tom together. When the grown-ups were finished eating, we took over the table and played a game of Monopoly. Surprisingly, we had a good time. When Tom got his nose out of his comic books, he was pretty nice. Since Marcy was the banker, she didn't have time to talk about makeup or boys.

Not until later, when everyone had gone home, did I really have time to think about the trick we had pulled. For Jerimy and me to travel with the clock was one thing. At least we had made the choice and knew there were risks. Marcy and Tom, on the other hand, had been in danger without even knowing it. The more I thought about what we had done, the worse I felt. Jerimy was bothered, too, because shortly after Mom and Dad went to bed, he knocked softly at my door.

"I couldn't sleep," he admitted. "I kept thinking about this afternoon."

"Me, too."

"Time traveling with Marcy and Tom was a dumb thing to do. Someone could have been hurt, and it would have been all my fault."

"Mine, too. I didn't say no."

"I didn't give you much of a chance. I told you to be careful and not use it, and then I did a stupid thing like that," Jerimy said.

"I've been thinking, Jerimy," I said. "You were right. As

long as we have the clock, we will be tempted to time travel, maybe even take others with us. Even if we don't, sooner or later something will happen. At least we got a chance to go back once, even though I didn't get to pick up an antique."

Jerimy looked thoughtful. "What about Eliza Jane? I know you wanted to see her again, and we did sort of promise. I would like to tell her she is our great-great-great-grandmother."

I smiled at Jerimy, happy to know that he wanted to see Eliza Jane as much as I did.

"OK," I said, "but that's it. For sure this time. I wish we knew why Mr. Z gave the clock to us, but I guess we will never know.

"I'm glad we got a chance to meet Mart and Eliza Jane, though," I sighed.

Jerimy and I promised each other that this would be our last trip. First we had to find out where to go. We had no idea where Eliza Jane might have lived when she was grown, although we did have one clue. We knew that she had married a shopkeeper, and her son had moved back to the farm. That meant she had stayed in Crystal Springs, at least. But where? The logical place to find out was at Grandpa's house. Although Jerimy wasn't very happy about visiting Grandpa, we went the next day after school.

"Well, isn't this nice," said Grandpa when he opened the door. "My two favorite visitors. It's been a long time since you've come. I've been working," he said, waving at his desk. It was piled high with stacks of letters, pictures, and old newspaper clippings.

"How about a glass of milk and some cookies?" Grandpa suggested. "I need a break myself."

"You need a secretary," I joked, straightening his desk.

"I think you're right," Grandpa laughed. "I would hire you, but secretaries wear dresses. Don't you ever wear anything but jeans?"

"I put on a dress almost every time I come," I protested, "even though jeans are comfortable. I look dumb riding a bike in a dress."

Grandpa sighed. "I don't know what's wrong with young people today. The boys don't want to be boys, but the girls do."

Suddenly, I saw red. "I have a friend at school, Grandpa. Her grandfather is kind of plump and jolly and brings her a present every time he comes. Now that's my idea of a grandpa. Why can't you be like that?"

There was a moment of shocked silence. Even Jerimy looked amazed. Finally, Grandpa cleared his throat. "Is that what I've been doing?"

"Yes," I said, still angry. "You spend so much time worrying about what I have on, or if Jerimy is going to play sports because you like sports, that you haven't taken the time to really know us. Jerimy may not like baseball, but he did win first prize at the science fair. You haven't even asked about it. He'll probably grow up and invent something wonderful.

"I love to collect antiques, which may come as a surprise to you because you don't even seem to care that I love history. All you care about is how I dress and wear my hair. That's only a part of me."

I stopped and took a deep breath, surprised by what I had said. I don't know what had finally given me the courage to speak up. Perhaps it was Jerimy's help. Or maybe it was thinking about Mart's people, afraid to stand up and speak out against the robots. Whatever it was, I felt relieved. Grandpa wasn't the sort of man many people would stand up to, but, at least, he knew how I felt. I hoped he wouldn't be too angry. I held my breath and waited. All my anger was gone.

Grandpa looked very upset. "You are both very dear to me, don't you know that? No, how could you? I've been so busy being a grumpy old man, I didn't even know I was making you unhappy. I guess I thought if I harped on it long enough, Jerimy would play sports, and love it because I do. And because I like to see girls in dresses, I thought it was right for you." He put his arms around us and led us to the kitchen. He poured some milk in glasses and set a plate of cookies out on the table. "Now, let's talk. Let's really get to know each other."

We talked until dinner time. Grandpa told us stories about his childhood, and Jerimy explained some of his projects. Grandpa even said he would go antique hunting with me. For the first time we really felt close.

"I guess old people need to learn things, too," Grandpa

said at last. "We can get stuck in our ways. This project of mine just makes it worse. All this thinking about the past is not good. I didn't know what I was getting into when I started collecting," he smiled. "It began as a little project to keep me busy. I also hoped that someday you two might be interested in our family's history."

"We're interested now," I said. Jerimy and I had already agreed not to tell Grandpa what we were looking for. Although he could probably tell us, we didn't want to give away why we were so interested in Eliza Jane.

Grandpa looked surprised. "Do you want to look through some of this stuff?"

"Just the things about our family," Jerimy quickly responded.

"I thought you were the one who didn't care about people. Didn't you tell me family history was boring?"

Jerimy gave him a mischievous smile. "I can change my mind, can't I?"

Grandpa grunted, but I could see he was pleased. "Most of the things in that box there cover our family. You can take it in the other room and look through it if you like."

Jerimy and I jumped at the chance. The box was full of old letters, photographs, and trinkets. In only a few minutes I had found an old picture of Eliza Jane and her husband, both looking stern and dignified. The picture was a little faded, but there was something oddly familiar about Eliza Jane's husband, the man who was our great-great-great-grandfather.

I gasped. "Did Mom say what Eliza Jane's husband's name was?"

"It was Fenton, same as ours," Jerimy said, looking up impatiently from an old letter he was reading.

"I don't mean that. I mean his first name. Do you suppose it was George?"

Jerimy looked a little green. "Let me see that!" He grabbed the picture out of my hand. "How could she marry him? Do you realize that means I had a fight with my great-grandfather?" he groaned.

"Great-great-great-grandfather," I giggled. "It sure looks that way. But at least he won."

"What do you mean?" Jerimy looked insulted. "He didn't win."

"You were the one with a black eye," I reminded him.

"He would have had one, too, if Mr. Weatherby hadn't come along. Maybe it was a tie, but he didn't win."

"This makes Mr. Weatherby our great-great-great-great-grandfather," I said.

Jerimy went back to the letters, while I continued to search the box. Suddenly, he gave a shout. "I've got it."

"What is it?" I asked.

"It's a letter from Dad's mother to one of our relatives. Most of it is just ordinary stuff, but listen to this. 'We worry about Great-Grandmother Eliza Jane. She hardly ever leaves her house anymore. Although we have tried to talk her into living with us, she refuses. I am glad her house is only a short way up the road so we can check on her now and then. I just got back, as a matter of fact, and found her well and baking a batch of cookies.'"

"Is there a date on the letter?"

"March 9, 1957," Jerimy said, checking the postmark.

"Let's make that the day we go," I said. "After we visit her, we can go by the farm. Maybe we can see Dad." I did some quick figuring. "He would have been just about our age then."

Jerimy laughed. "Remember what he said about going back and seeing his dad? Now we're going to do that to him!"

"It would be great to talk to him, but we'd better not. He might look at us some day and remember," I said.

Grandpa came in the room. "Did you two find anything interesting?"

"Yeah, we did," Jerimy said. "By the way, Grandpa, I think I know a way this might be easier."

"I'm all ears," Grandpa said.

"Why don't you get a big board and put up a sheet of paper for each person in the main families? That way, you could keep track of them a little easier and move them around as they get married or die," he suggested. Grandpa looked at him strangely.

"What's the matter? I was just trying to help," Jerimy said.

Grandpa seemed to shake himself awake. "I'm sorry. For a minute I thought of something that happened long ago." He looked confused. Shaking his head, he laughed.

"It was silly. Now, about your idea—I think it's great. You wouldn't know anyone who might want to help set it up, would you?"

"I would," Jerimy and I answered together. "We both would," Jerimy added. "That is, if you want us to."

"I think that would be wonderful," Grandpa said. "Nothing like a little work together to get to know a person. Besides, I imagine a scientist is pretty good at cataloging information," he grinned.

"You know," he said, turning to me. "As I was working just now, I thought of something. There were a lot of strong women in our family, just like you, Julie. They might have worn dresses, but they worked right beside the men. One of them even held off some Indians when her husband was away. Won, too!"

I couldn't help but laugh.

Jerimy and I were in a pretty good mood by the time we left Grandpa's house. We were even happier when we looked up March 9, 1957, in the perpetual calendar in the almanac and discovered it was a Saturday.

"Perfect," I exclaimed gleefully. "We can ride our bikes to school tomorrow, and when we go back to 1957, we will have a way out to the farm without looking suspicious. We will be just a couple of kids out for a bike ride."

"But after we see Eliza Jane, we are coming back to our time and staying there," Jerimy said sternly.

I sighed and nodded. I knew there could be no more

101

trips through time, but I couldn't help feeling sad.

"By the way," Jerimy said a bit awkwardly, "thanks for what you said about me to Grandpa. I couldn't believe it was you, saying all those things."

"I couldn't, either," I grinned. "But I guess you were right. A person has to stick up for herself once in a while. Anyhow, I think it worked. Grandpa really seemed to understand."

"You also showed me that you can't tell people how you really feel unless you care about them. You showed me, Julie, that I really do care about people, especially Grandpa."

I went to bed, feeling great about the way things were working out. But it was hard to remain cheerful when I got up the next morning and saw the weather. The skies were dark and overcast, promising rain or even snow. For a few minutes I thought Mom was going to insist that we take the bus to school. "Are you sure you want to ride your bikes today?" she asked. She frowned as she gazed out the window.

"We need the exercise," I said quickly.

Twenty minutes later, we were riding down a country road on a beautiful spring morning. The sun was warm on our backs as we peddled, and the leaves were beginning to bud on the trees. Even the air had a heavenly spring smell.

Several cars passed as we rode, but no one gave us a second glance. Except that the cars were an older style, everything looked about the same as it did in our time. Many of the houses we recognized, but now, of course, they looked newer.

Finding our way was easy. There were only a few houses on the road, and the third one had "Fenton" neatly stenciled on the mailbox. Sitting back off the road was a large, homey farmhouse, and behind the house was a large red barn. I watched as we rode past, but there was no one in sight. As we rounded a curve in the road, I noticed a small white cottage nestled in the trees. I knew, even before we saw the name on the mailbox, that this was Eliza Jane's home.

Jerimy put his hand on my arm. "I just thought of something. Maybe we should have tried to find her when she was younger. Maybe she won't remember us. After all, she is over ninety. Old people forget things."

I shook my head. "Not Eliza Jane. She'll remember."

"Well, there is only one way to find out," Jerimy said, turning into the drive.

Anxious now, I parked my bike next to Jerimy's under the trees and headed for the door. Without hesitating, I knocked. For a long minute nothing happened, and I feared we had picked the wrong day after all. Finally, the door opened a crack, and someone peeked out.

The face at the door was wrinkled and old, and the hair was completely white, but there was no mistaking those sparkling blue eyes. All our worry disappeared in the next minute, for the woman threw open the door and, grinning broadly, wrapped her arms around us.

"You remembered," she exclaimed in a voice that was still Eliza Jane's. "I've waited and watched for you all my life. I knew I would see you again. Now, at last, you are here."

12 A Rescue and an Explanation

"So we've decided to throw away the clock," Jerimy said after we told Eliza Jane the story. "But, first, we wanted to see you."

"I'm so glad you did. To find out you are my very own family! That makes it all the more wonderful. George would have loved the joke," she said, her eyes misty.

We had already learned from Grandpa's family history that George had died twenty years earlier. We sat in Eliza Jane's small, bright, pretty kitchen, eating freshly baked cookies as we talked.

"It's been a long time since I baked cookies," Eliza Jane said. "I must have had second sight that you were coming."

A red checkered tablecloth covered the table, and there were matching curtains at the windows, which were lined with flowering plants. The scent of flowers mingled with the warm cinnamon from the cookies. I leaned back comfortably in my chair. "How did you happen to marry George? I thought you didn't like him."

Eliza Jane had a faraway look in her eyes. "George always felt bad about that fight. You see, he liked me even then, and I am afraid he was a little jealous. But he turned out to be a fine young man, and, of course, we had a secret to share."

She laughed suddenly. "Do you remember how I admired your shoes?" She pointed to the bright blue sneakers she wore. "They are so comfortable. It was worth the wait until they started making them."

"We have to go," Jerimy said reluctantly. "We wanted to take a peek at Dad when he was our age, and then we have to get back to our own time and go to school."

"What a shame. Your father isn't here today. He is over in Marysville playing the regional championship game. You could take a peek at the farm if you are interested. Just climb through the woods up that hill," she directed. "You can get a good look, and no one is likely to spot you."

I could have told her that the Crystal Springs team had won the championship that day, but I didn't want to spoil the surprise. "Good-bye, Grandma," I said awkwardly.

She chuckled as she kissed our cheeks. "You just remember me as your friend, Eliza Jane."

It was already late afternoon. We waved good-bye and trudged up the hill she had pointed out, disappointed that we wouldn't be seeing Dad. Jerimy stopped and rested against a tree. "Do you realize that we have been up a whole day, and we still have a long ride before we get to school?"

"It was worth it," I said. "Don't you think so?"

Jerimy nodded. "There's the farm," he said, pointing.

From where we stood, the farm spread out like a picture postcard. Neatly plowed fields, ready for spring planting, stretched out in every direction, and a dog napped in the afternoon sun. Even as we watched, the dog got up and eagerly ran to meet the man coming from the house.

"That must be Grandpa," Jerimy said. "He looks a lot younger."

We watched as the man stopped to pet the dog, then walked quickly to the barn.

"I'll bet he is going to the barn to do the afternoon milking," Jerimy said. "Come on. He will probably be in the barn for quite a while. We might as well leave."

"Wait," I cried. "Who is that?"

A man ran out of the barn and slammed the door. He paused for a moment, then slid the bar on the door down, locking it, and ran off towards the woods.

"What's going on?" Jerimy asked. "Why do you suppose he did that?"

I grabbed his arm. "Don't you recognize him? That's Mr. Z." Suddenly, something clicked in the back of my mind—something Dad had told us about his childhood.

"Oh, my gosh," I screamed. "The fire. Remember? Dad said an old bum locked him in the barn."

Even as I spoke, a thin trickle of smoke curled up from the barn roof. Frantically, we raced down the hill to our bikes. Eliza Jane was still out on her porch.

"Call the fire department. There's a fire at the farm," I yelled.

Without waiting to see if she understood, we pedaled our bikes back down the road and flew around the curve. By this time, flames were shooting out from the side of the barn.

"Quick," Jerimy gasped. "Help me lift the bar." Together we pushed it up and swung open the door. Thick black smoke rolled out, making our eyes water and choking us.

Grandpa stumbled out, holding a handkerchief over his nose and sputtering.

"You saved my life. Call the fire department. I've got to get those cows out," he wheezed.

"They are already coming," I said, just as we heard the first thin wail of the fire trucks turning off the main road.

"Help me get the cows, boy," Grandpa yelled, stumbling back inside the barn.

Jerimy started to follow, but I took his arm. "Look, the firemen are here. We know all the cows are saved, but Grandpa isn't supposed to find out who we are or see us long enough to remember our faces. We'd better get out of here."

Jerimy nodded. "You're right," he said, backing away from the noise and confusion. No one noticed as we grabbed our bikes and headed back to the road. Nervously, I set the clock and sent us back to our own time.

"Do you realize what just happened?" Jerimy panted. "We were the ones who saved Grandpa that day. Mr. Z gave us the clock so we could save our own grandpa."

"That's right," rasped a voice from the side of the road. A familiar figure stepped out of the bushes.

"Why didn't you just tell us what we were supposed to do?" I demanded.

"Because I didn't know why you were there. You were there for another reason. I only knew you would end up at the farm, somehow, once you had the clock."

"What do you mean, you knew we would be there?" I asked. "How could you know what we would do?"

"Because I saw you there nearly thirty years ago." He paused, letting that sink in before he continued. "When I saw the fire that day, I tried to run back and unlock the door. But I tripped and twisted my ankle. I couldn't make it back to the barn. As I lay there, horrified at what I had done, I saw you two ride up and unlock the door."

"But we wouldn't have been there unless you gave us the clock," I protested.

"Even I didn't know that until I saw you that day in the marketplace," said Mr. Z. "I had assumed you were neighbor children who just happened by. But when I saw you, it all became clear. I knew I had to give you the clock and let you find your own way. It was meant to be, you see."

Mr. Z smiled, and he no longer seemed so fearful. He looked like what he was—a tired old man.

"When I first invented the clock, I only wanted to study

history at first hand. Like you, Julie, I liked to collect things from the past. And like you, Jerimy, I was interested in science. Yes," he nodded, "I know a great deal about you. I didn't mean to frighten you, but I had to make sure you were the right ones. So I watched and waited."

"You did scare me," I said sharply.

"I know. And I am sorry. But I had to make certain. In the wrong hands, the clock could be disastrous. But I'm sure you've realized that yourselves. That's why the clock wasn't working when I gave it to you. I knew if I was right, you would fix it. I knew I had to be the one to give you the clock, since it hadn't been invented in your day. I couldn't just tell you to go. You would have thought I was a crazy old man, and I didn't know what events had brought you to that spot."

"Eliza Jane," Jerimy and I said together.

"But how did you happen to come to our time? Besides, we were told that all the clocks had been destroyed," Jerimy continued.

"After I invented the clock, I traveled the world, meeting famous people and watching the world grow. Then I made clocks so that others could go, too. The Director and the council wanted to outlaw time travel. They said it was too dangerous for humans, that they would be careless and change time. I argued that time could not be changed, at least not in any important way. That what is meant to be, will be. But of course, I was wrong.

"I kept traveling back in time. One day as I traveled

down a country road, I became weary. I decided to sneak into a barn for a rest. Foolishly, I lit my pipe. I thought I had safely put it out before I went to sleep. When I woke up and heard your grandfather in the barn, I panicked. I locked the door to give myself time to get away. I returned to my own time ashamed of what I had done. The Director ordered all the clocks destroyed and ordered me banished to another time," said Mr. Z.

"But you didn't start the fire," Jerimy said. "Dad told us the fire marshal determined that the fire was started by faulty wiring."

Mr. Z stared at Jerimy for a minute. "Then in a sense, there was no crime. Perhaps I can go back. Perhaps the Director can be convinced to allow me to spend my last years among my friends."

"You still didn't explain how you happen to have a clock. Mart told us they were all destroyed," I said.

"The Director wanted to make certain I wouldn't simply make a new clock, once they were all destroyed. There is an element that will not be discovered for a hundred years. In this time period, I would not live long enough to see it discovered. But I managed to smuggle out enough for one clock. Maybe it was an accident that the Director chose this time as my banishment, but maybe it was something more. Perhaps you could call it fate, bringing time to a full circle."

"The capsule in the time clock," Jerimy said. "I wondered what it was. That's the element, isn't it?"

Mr. Z nodded. "There you are again. Since you are interested in science, you were curious and wanted to fix the clock. And your sister wanted to travel and see the history she loves. Was that fate again?" Mr. Z shrugged. "I think we will not know those answers. You two have simply traveled through time, and perhaps become a little wiser.

"But what if I had not given you the clock? Would fate have intervened to see that your grandfather was saved? I don't know the answer. What I do know is that I am going to destroy the clock when I return to my rightful time. The human race will not be ready for time travel until we have learned much more about time and destiny."

I smiled at Mr. Z, and touched his dry, leathery hand. "Will you be all right?"

"I think so," he said. "But it doesn't really matter. I am an old man and have lived a full life. I only hope I will be able to tell my people what I have seen in other times. Some good, some bad, but always people in control of their own destiny."

"Wait," I cried. "There is one more thing that bothers me. You said you were studying history. But nothing very important ever happened in Crystal Springs. How did you happen to be here in 1957?"

Mr. Z set the time clock. For a minute I thought he wasn't going to answer. Then a faint smile crossed his face. "It was a little personal project. You see, my dear, I was studying my family tree. I am one of your direct descendants." He raised his hand in farewell and was gone, leaving us alone, standing in a cold October rain. This time we knew he was gone forever.

I sighed, looking at the dreary sky. Then I looked at my watch and groaned. "We could use that clock one more time," I shouted uselessly to the wind. "It's cold, and we are going to be late for school."

13 A Gift from the Past

We had to stay after school that night.

"Do you have an excuse for being so late?" Mrs. Rollins, our teacher, asked.

"We do," Jerimy shrugged. "But you would never believe it."

Mrs. Rollins didn't seem to like that answer. She added half an hour to a day that was already two days long. As soon as we got home, Jerimy and I both headed for our rooms and collapsed on our beds. It took a lot of talking to convince Mom we weren't coming down with something.

Life sort of settled down after that. Jerimy went back to inventing things, but not a time clock, of course. It was about a thousand years too soon. Mom and Dad went back to complaining about the mess in Jerimy's room, and I got a *D* on my next math test. Jerimy and I made a few friends. Now that he makes a little more effort to get to know people, others are discovering what I knew all along—he is a pretty nice person and a good friend.

Marcy and Tom came back one day and tried to talk us into the "game." They were unhappy when we refused, but we made up a story about having a hard time waking someone up. I guess they believed us. After that, Marcy went back to talking about makeup and boys, and Tom retreated back to his comic books. We might have been friends one day—they weren't really that bad—but they moved not long after, and we never saw them again.

Sometime it seemed as if our time travels had never happened, that it was just a dream. Jerimy and I walked past the empty store where Mr. Z had given us the clock, but it remained empty and closed. Then one day the building was torn down. A sign said it was going to be a parking lot.

"I wish we could tell someone," Jerimy said. "But who would ever believe us? You never even got your antique. That might have helped."

One thing that had changed was our relationship with Grandpa. We continued to help him with his book, and now even Jerimy loved to go over to his house. Every once in a while he would look at us strangely, and I knew he was remembering a day long ago. But he never mentioned it, and neither did we. Of course, Grandpa was still Grandpa. There were days when he griped that he never saw me in a dress, or that he didn't have any reason to watch the ball games. But now we just laugh, and call him old-fashioned, and he laughs and agrees.

One day when we went over to help sort through another box, we found Grandpa sitting at his desk in the study, with a puzzled look on his face.

"I found the strangest thing," he said, before he had even said hello.

"Uh, oh," Jerimy joked, "one of our ancestors was a horse thief?"

"I found this box," Grandpa said. "There is a letter saying that it is to be given to you. But I'm sure the box has been in storage since before you were born."

Jerimy gave me a nudge. It was the same box where we had found the letter. Yet surely we would have noticed a package that day.

"Who is it from?" I asked, confused.

"That's the strange part," Grandpa said. "It's from your great-great-great-grandmother, Eliza Jane, and it has your names on it. But she died fifteen years before you were born. How could she have known what your names would be, or even that you would exist?"

Jerimy looked at me. "Maybe she was psychic," he offered feebly.

"I've been sitting here all afternoon, and that's as good an explanation as any I came up with," Grandpa said. He gave us that odd look again and shook his head. "Beats me," he said. "Well, open it up, and see what it is."

I felt the hairs on the back of my neck start to prickle.

Grandpa came over to the couch with us. We tore open the outer coverings, yellow and dry with age. Inside was a small box for each of us. I felt sad as well as excited as

I opened mine. Something slipped out and fell to the floor. I picked it up and caught my breath. It was a locket, very small, very old, and very beautiful. I remembered that Eliza Jane had worn it to a Fourth of July celebration long ago. A tiny clasp was on one side. Carefully, I pressed it open with a fingernail. Inside were two faded pictures. On one side was George, a mischievous grin on his face. On the other side was Eliza Jane, looking very much like the day we first met. "Always friends" read the tiny engraving on the edge.

"It's lovely," I sighed. "I'll keep it forever."

"I think that's a picture of my great-grandmother and grandfather," Grandpa said, squinting at the picture. "I don't suppose the pictures mean much to you, but the locket is very old and probably very valuable."

"Oh, no," I said, holding it tightly in my hand, "I love having the pictures, too."

Grandpa gave me another one of his strange looks, and I wondered if it would really hurt to tell him the story. Maybe we would, someday. Grandpa turned to Jerimy. "What is in your package?"

A beautiful antique watch lay in Jerimy's palm. "It's engraved, too," he said softly.

"What does it say?" Grandpa asked.

"It says," Jerimy answered with a smile, "'Time is on your side. Fill it with love.'"

About the Author

Bonnie Pryor resides in Mt. Vernon, Ohio, with her husband and is the mother of five children. Although she has worked in a variety of interesting occupations, such as sandblasting, and in unusual places, a fireworks factory, Ms. Pryor now concentrates her time on writing and caring for her two youngest children.

She wrote *Mr. Z and the Time Clock*, not only as a fun book to read, but to emphasize the importance of family relationships and to help children understand the part that they play in changing themselves and their world.

Ms. Pryor has written picture books and numerous magazine articles. *Mr. Z and the Time Clock* is her first novel.